BLINDFOLD

BLINDFOLD

SANDRA McCUAIG

Holiday House / New York

Library of Congress Cataloging-in-Publication Data

McCuaig, Sandra.
Blindfold / by Sandra McCuaig.
p.   cm.
Summary: Benji and his blind older brother Joel share a very
special bond until their suicide, leaving feelings of grief and
guilt with fifteen-year-old friend Sally.
ISBN 0-8234-0811-6
[1. Brothers—Fiction.   2. Suicide—Fiction.   3. Blind—Fiction.
4. Physically handicapped—Fiction.   5. Friendship—Fiction.]
I. Title
PZ7.M13864B1   1990   89-24509   CIP   AC
[Fic]—dc20

BLINDFOLD

1

The first time I saw the name Dr Jago I was suspicious. It was written on our kitchen wall calendar in the Tuesday square, the 22nd of March, with the time underlined: 4.30.

My sixth sense told me it had something to do with me, not that *she* would say so if I asked.

Tessa (that is what I call my mum) is secretive these days. She kind of blames me for what happened. She says I've got the answers everybody needs to know. But really I don't understand why it happened any more than she does.

She says (and I guess this whole damn town would agree) that there has to be a reason behind the tragedy. Someone has to be responsible. And that someone, in everyone's mind, is me.

Today is the marked Tuesday, and Tessa was more agitated than usual as she prepared to leave for work this morning.

'You will go to school today,' she said, knowing I might not, 'and meet me at this address at 4.30.'

1

She handed me a piece of paper.

I stared at her, indignant, for even then she did not say who he was. Dr Jago, I mean. She just looked at me, shaking her head. Her big brown eyes seemed squeezed by tight muscles, her little face a picture of pain framed with auburn curls.

'I give up, I give up!' she despaired and swirled on her high heels. 'Just you be there.'

So here I am, because, I suppose, I don't want Tessa to suffer any more. These two months since it happened have been hell for lots of people. If I hadn't been born Tessa would have had a simple, happy life. It can't be any fun living with someone 'the devil has got into' (her words).

The address on the piece of paper was Link Street, commonly known as Shrink Street, so it was no surprise to read on the polished brass sign at the entrance to the building:

Dr P. D. JAGO, PSYCHIATRIST.

Tessa is already there when I arrive, pacing up and down.

'Why are you so late?' are her first words. 'You're the reason we're here, and you're late.'

And after a pause she adds, 'As usual these days, you have nothing to say. Soon you'll be talking, though. This Dr Jago won't put up with your silence.'

I look up and see the doctor standing in the doorway to his consulting room, listening to her outburst. He isn't wearing a white coat like they do in mental hospitals on television. No, he looks just like someone's dad.

When Tessa spots him, she kind of jumps, embarrassed I think, when she realises he had heard her going on. Dr Jago just smiles and beckons us in. He's got a funny smile. It starts very slowly and creeps up his cheeks, and then stays on his face while he talks. It doesn't look bad, mind you. It's kind of right for his face.

'Come in. The most important person can have my new armchair,' he says.

Tessa avoids the armchair and perches, back so straight, on an upright chair far from his desk.

I also avoid the armchair and take a firm stand by the window.

Tessa takes an audibly deep breath (a habit she has developed lately) holds it for a bit, then launches into her explanation for our visit. She talks like a rushing river.

'Well, doctor, we're here because something awful happened and nothing is the same any more. Sally and I used to be so close, but she's troubled now, so troubled. Things aren't right for us. She skips school. We can't talk any more. Sally and I . . . we were best friends. But what happened is now ruining everything. This is . . .'

I can feel Dr Jago watching me even though I am looking out the window. Tessa's voice is going on. It's a kind of background noise to my private world inside my head.

3

Dr Jago's voice butts in, 'Hey, Sally, is my new fangle-dangle chair a waste of money? Have I been had by those fancy decorator people? They told me no one could resist that chair. Try it. Tell me what you think.'

I don't move. Not even an eyelash.

He sits in the chair himself and starts trying the buttons, which rearrange him into a succession of ridiculous positions.

Now he is in one which, from the corner-of-my-eye point of view, best exposes his hairy nostrils. He asks, 'How about this one?'

Tessa is fidgeting. She insists on being heard. 'You see, doctor, she hasn't got a father, and if he had stayed around we wouldn't have to be here. I can't do it all. I can't be expected to do it all—work all day and cope with these problems. You see, Sally's got real problems, doctor, all because . . .'

I think she stopped talking because Dr Jago got up. I didn't want to hear those words she was going to say, and I'm glad he didn't seem to either.

Dr Jago is now standing beside me at the window. He, too, is watching the traffic below. Seven floors below. That would be enough to do it. Seven floors and it would all be over like it was for Benji and Joel.

Down on the street there is an argument going on between some old wrinkly and a guy—she has backed her car right into his parked motorbike and now has it hooked on her bumper-bar. It would be funny listening to her excuses, stupid bitch.

But I'm not down there, in the real world. I'm up

here in this nutcracker's suite. And there is no way I am going to sit on that chair—it makes Dr Jago look a real lunatic. Perhaps he is!

He speaks. His voice sounds distant, even though he is right beside me.

'Come now. We're going to be friends. Why don't you take my seat behind the desk and I'll rest in that comfortable chair.'

As if in a dream, I take his seat. The writing pad on the desk has nothing on it, just my name:

Sally O'Leary, age 15.

Really I should add Tessa's name, 'cos we're both screwed up, if you ask me.

But then no one is going to ask me, because I'm *The Problem* . . . the living, breathing reason for the tragedy. I am responsible for their deaths, so they say. And maybe they are right. Have I got 'fatal charm'? Am I a witch?

Dr Jago is saying, 'Counselling, talking out problems, is the way we help our patients unravel their feelings, understand what they do and why they do it. Talking is a healing process that doesn't hurt. Keep in mind that people come to doctors, like myself, not because they can't cope with their lives, but because they want to better understand their situations.'

What would he know about love, I wonder? He looks like a goof. Imagine kissing that moustache! All prickles, no passion. Uggh! I'm not telling him about Benji, or Joel. For sure. And nothing he could do or say will make things the way they were.

'I have no magic formula,' he admits. 'You will find the answers by yourself with my guidance. We will explore together. Discovering the answers will be gradual. We will try to make sense of it all and find some inner peace.

'Every mind,' he continues, 'is troubled at some time. We all have a worry or two.'

A worry, he calls it! He's an idiot. He couldn't even begin to understand.

Dr Jago adds, 'I'm sure we'll find some of the answers you are looking for.'

No one speaks. The quiet is so loud.

Tessa is restless. She has crossed and uncrossed her legs nine million times and cleared her throat once more. I know she's dying to blab, but she can't bring herself to break the silence.

Dr Jago finds a new position on his mobile chair.

I stare at the pad with my name on it.

After what seems like forever Dr Jago says, 'So let's start our conversation, eh, Sally? What are the best times for you to visit? I'd like to see you both, separately at first, and on a regular basis. Say twice a week, till we get to understand each other? How would that fit in?' he enquires.

Tessa is rustling some rather crumpled newspaper pages. I know what they are.

She pipes up, 'Sure. I can drive her here. She

needs help quickly. I worry that she might . . .'

Dr Jago cuts in, 'Fine. Write twice a week down for me, dear one, on that writing pad in front of you.'

He is talking to me, again. Without looking up, I write: 'NEVER NEVER', in my biggest writing. He couldn't see the pad from where he lounged, but he must have read my hand movements like people read lips.

He says, 'I understand, Sally. It's up to you. But what about a little try?'

I feel so small. Tessa can't know what has happened. She sits on the edge of her chair, gripping the newspaper cuttings, her throat freshly cleared, her mouth at the ready.

Now she is going to take her chance. I dread it. I wish I were dead. She thrusts the papers at Dr Jago, imploring, 'She's the girl. You see, she's the girl.'

I watch him open the crumpled pages, smooth them, and nod slowly as if there is a lot to read. There is nothing much, just eight words and a picture of a lighthouse:

YOUNG BROTHERS
JUMP TO DEATHS:
LOVED SAME GIRL

2

Tessa's old friends say I'm the dead spit of her when she was a girl. If that's the case, then there is hope for me. First of all, I am looking forward to my hair fading. At the moment it is orange; no other word for it. In fact, to be quite honest, I should say bright orange. I keep it together with rubber bands most of the time, and when I let it loose it flares out something like one of those wild flames that shoot out of an oil well on fire.

People pat my hair when they sit behind me in the cinema. They think I can't feel their curious touch. Little kids love the bouncy curls and they often stick their little hands inside the thick mass as if they were looking for a surprise . . . a small bird perhaps?

I would have had it cut right off long ago, except that so many people say it is 'my crowning glory', and there is nothing else about me that they ever comment on. Fair enough. My face is freckled, my teeth are not yet straight (they will be if Mum can find the money; she'd better hurry up) and there is simply nothing else to notice about me.

Tessa and I haven't spoken at all about Dr Jago. She thinks it will all work out her way, that I'll get palsy-walsy with him and tell him all.

I beat my pillow at night when I think about him. I hate him, I hate him, I hate him! She thinks I'm going to spend hours in that awful, stuffy room, but she's got another think coming.

I don't want to see anyone. I'm better off by myself. Kate, I suppose, *was* my best friend, but now she is so nosy.

Mrs Barratt (my teacher) has turned into a proper bitch. She rings Tessa every day I think—Sally was late, Sally wasn't at school today, Sally didn't eat her lunch, Sally's not mixing well. I could kill her. Why doesn't she mind her *own* business. What's it to her if I *want* to fail.

I'm so glad I've got Miaow. That's all my cat says, but she is the best person to talk to. Seems to know everything. And the knowing doesn't make any difference to our friendship.

Since Benji and Joel did what they did, everyone I know has changed. They won't leave me alone.

Tessa is calling. 'Time to go, Sally. It will take fifteen minutes to get to Dr Jago's and we don't want to be late.'

She seems to talk to herself these days and doesn't seem to mind if no one answers.

As she drives, she says, 'Time means money. I wouldn't mind his job. Chat, chat all day.'

9

She does chat, chat all day, and I should know. I'd pay not to hear her most of the time. She is speeding to Dr Jago, the man who she hopes will change everything. I think that is why she is cheerful.

In Dr Jago's room, the manic chair has been banished to the far corner. In its place is a battered leather armchair, with another well-worn comfortable one close by.

Dr Jago is wearing his smile. I don't speak when spoken to. He seems happy enough babbling on to himself.

'We're going to do some games today. We won't talk about anything personal. I've got a few exercises here that are quite a challenge, not easy, but I think you will enjoy doing them while I get on with some paperwork.'

Dr Jago gives me some instructions and returns to his desk.

I do the puzzles. Nothing else to do. They were easy. I don't know what he was on about.

Then he gets out some really amazing drawings and asks me to describe them. They are weirdo. One of his really mad patients must have done them. I tell him so. He asks me why and I give it to him just like our art teacher, Mrs Drummond, would have if I had handed in something so crazy.

I say, 'Anyone who paints with those colours, all mixed up like that, must be painting a nightmare. I've seen that sort of thing, but only in my head, at night, especially after I've cried myself to sleep.

'They are hideous,' I tell him straight.

There are some nice ones someone had done by imagining a jungle. Plenty of animals in the pictures, sleeping and eating. He tells me I saw more than he had ever seen before. (Even with the help of the madman who painted it, I wonder?)

Then I point out the bats, lots of bats. They can't see, and they fly around blind just listening for clues so they don't bash into things.

Dr Jago finds that interesting. He writes notes on his writing pad when I talk about the bats.

'Tell me,' he asks, 'have you seen many bats?'

'Not really. But I kind of know what it would feel like to be blind, 'cos sometimes I pretend to be.'

'Is that fun?' he asks.

I have to tell him. 'It used to be. I don't do it any more.'

3

Untoasted muesli is absolutely disgusting. My stomach has to be tricked into taking every mouthful. I chew, add more milk, chew more, add more milk . . . and then force it down.

Tessa says raw food is best and that chewing develops strong jaws. Suppose I'll need them if I'm going to survive on her home-made muesli.

This morning I was working hard on a mouthful when I suddenly noticed my name and Dr Jago's name written together on the calendar in today's square. Panic. My heart started banging inside . . . 'Let me out, let me out' . . . and every neon nerve in my body seemed to burn red hot.

Tessa was chatting at the time. She was in the kitchen with me, but I don't think she saw the light—the searchlight that came through the calendar and pinned me down. It was a riveting white light, so strong that I could not move out of it. I now know why rabbits and foxes and kangaroos stop still when their eyes are held by the night shooters' spotlight.

Bang. Tessa's hand slapped the wet sink. 'Will you stop dribbling milk down that clean uniform. You can go like that to school. I'm not going to provide you with two outfits a day.'

I was spared. But I felt tired as the fear died down. And cross. I saw Dr Jago only the day before yesterday. And you know how good that was for me. It was a waste of time, and money. He talked and I did puzzles. Honestly!

'Now you hurry along and sponge that spot off before you go,' said Tessa as she gathered her handbag, lipstick, two diet biscuits (her lunch), two tissues and one ironed, lace-trimmed linen handkerchief which I suspect she has just in case she cries in front of her boss.

'Dr Jago is expecting you this afternoon,' she said cheerfully. 'Such a nice man. I had such a friendly chat with him yesterday. He really knows how to help. I'll be waiting outside for you.'

She kissed me. 'Don't be late,' she said and hurried out the door. I watched her totter on her high heels. They make her look as if there are two forces of gravity at work—the second one pulls her upper body forward as if she were being pulled along by an imaginary lead.

I then realised I was too exhausted to go to school. All that muesli chewing didn't help. I had to have more rest before I would be able to concentrate.

I lay down beside Miaow. I don't know for how long, but I was definitely asleep when the phone started ringing. The first call was probably Mrs Barratt. And

13

I suspect the second time it rang was her again. I didn't answer it, of course.

The third time it rang I knew it was Tessa, alerted by that dobbing Mrs Barratt. I had to get out of the place. Tessa would soon be on her way and I'd get heaps. I couldn't hack it.

Out of the yukky uniform, into a pair of jeans, off down the street, just as far away from our house as I could get. I had a few dollars, so I bought a drink and went down to the rock ledge at the northern end of the beach.

My friend was there. And he was in a talking mood. Sometimes he is shut, just like a shop is shut—his body is there, but his mind's somewhere else.

I'm not scared of him. Some people are, but that's because they don't like dirt, and he carries a lot of it around on him. It's even in the pores of his skin, and if you magnified his face it would be like seeing lots of little black dots.

I call him Lifesaver. He likes that. It makes him smile—perhaps he is remembering how he was when he was young. He might have been clean and white then. He would not have been a jogger. His ankles sometimes peep out of his worn, torn trousers and I can't help looking at them—they are white and thin like birds' legs.

He's always been around this town, looking exactly the same. Most people think he is a nut, but he's not a drunk and he never hurts anything. In fact he saves sick seagulls.

When I first asked Tessa about him she said, 'Harmless hobo. Don't stare.'

She doesn't bother talking to him when she sees him. I do. This rock ledge where he sits is where I come when I don't want to go to school.

No one would look for me here. Lifesaver never asks me why I am the only person with school holidays. He just doesn't ask questions. And only sometimes will he answer them.

He has never admitted where he came by the huge trunk he keeps his everything in. It is mounted on the wheels of an old pram and is marked clearly: D. A. F. Hutchison-Marlowe, FIRST CLASS, A DECK, QUEEN MARY.

I don't think that is his real name.

Today he is reading the papers as usual. He must know a lot. His two one-legged seagulls are sitting (and shitting) on his trunk. He doesn't mind if they do that. Other people notice the poop and make fun of him.

I'd like to clean it off for him, but that might be interfering.

He doesn't look at me when I sit down, his eyes seem to be magnetised by the giant magnifying glass he passes over the day-old, grease-stained newspaper. As he reads, his head is drawn quickly back and forth across the print. I get the feeling that not a word goes unnoticed.

Eventually he folds it, puts it under his bum as a cushion and stares out to sea.

I put my school lunch beside him. The seagulls descend and squawk. He opens the brown paper bag, breaks up one sandwich for the birds and eats one himself.

'Lifesaver, are you very short-sighted?' I ask.

'Depends where I'm focused,' he replies.

Now, I ask myself, does that make sense? Sometimes Livesaver talks rot. He loves twisting words and making me ask more questions. 'What d'you mean? What d'you mean?' he keeps me saying.

He can be really annoying; either he is not there to talk to (that's when he's 'shut' and won't reply at all), or he carries on a mental merry-go-round.

'Can you see that ship on the horizon?' I persist.

'Well, now,' he shakes his head, still staring into the blue yonder. 'The truth is I can't quite see the particular vessel you speak of, but I can see right past it.'

'How can you see past it if you can't see it?' I insist.

'Some people can see what's beyond it all,' he explains. 'Some people know different planes of consciousness, different worlds of existence. There are more than five senses to "see" with and one day you might sense how to see forever.'

The ship I am watching is disappearing even though I have really good eyesight.

Lifesaver is in orbit. But I like him. The seagulls like him and I know there are some wild cats that trust him and no one else. I've seen him on this ledge with cats, but they go as soon as they see me.

His words are confusing but they mean something to him, that's for sure. I don't think he is just a mad mumbler, because he talks so definite, sort of like a brainy person.

And sometimes, for no reason, he laughs loudly. It's a shock when he does it, and poor One-leg One and One-leg Two (that's what we call his pet seagulls) get knocked off balance with fright. They take off and return when he has settled back to quiet nodding.

I think about what he had said as the seagulls circle. Then I tell him, 'I had a friend who said he had seen beyond this world and that there were better places to be. He was a blind boy.'

Lifesaver looks at me. His eyes are sharp when they stare. And the colour—it is hardly there, maybe pale blue, but a faraway colour, hidden in a crevice of his dirty, bearded face.

'And I suppose he heard voices no one else heard?' he asks.

'That's right,' I say. 'Voices from the outer universe. I knew you would understand, 'cos I've seen you talking to yourself as you walk around town, and sometimes you have a squeaky voice, and sometimes a big boomer.'

Lifesaver is thoughtful, then slaps the carry-all trunk, sending the seagulls off again.

In a commanding tone he insists, 'My voices are real; they don't come from outer space, they live right here.' He taps his tangled hair. 'They are earth-resident voices of spirit actors rehearsing a play on Life, spelt

17

with a capital L. I'm the director and they do as I tell them.'

We sit quietly for a while. What can you say to all that!

Then, like a bolt of lightning, he strikes me with these words, 'They say that one of those two boys that suicided near that lighthouse was blind, but they were *both* short-sighted, impatient little buggers hellbent on reaching heaven.

'Their action was selfish—they must have destroyed the souls of so many loved ones who are doing their time on earth.

'What's the world coming to when kids take on God's job?'

4

When the sun reaches a certain point on the ledge, Lifesaver reminds me that school is out, and I make my way home, doing the little jobs I am supposed to along the way.

I have to collect whatever Tessa has ordered over the phone from Mario, the greengrocer, and check our mail box at the Post Office.

Usually I don't even have to dig out the key, because the girls who work there know if we have something. I just catch their attention and they either shake or nod their heads.

Just as well they are so helpful, because I keep the key in my school uniform and there have been many days lately when I haven't had that on.

There is no point in going to school if you know you are not in a concentrating mood. There is no room in my brain for facts: it is jam-packed with worries. Maybe one day the worries will leave me (I don't know how or when) and I will be able to learn again.

In maths last week I got 14 out of 100 and I was

given a detention for today. Yes, today. That is another reason why I didn't want to go to school, because I think I know less maths now than I did last week.

And I haven't started the project on Italy. Anyway, that place must be near empty, there are so many Italians here.

Mario, the Friendly Fruitologist, has brought all his family here, and his wife's family, brothers, sisters, cousins, aunts. They joke that they 'make a Little Italy here', in our part of town.

Now, that's a thought . . . I could tell Mrs Barratt when I next go to school that I have been researching Italian customs locally.

It will be a brand new excuse. I've used up every imaginable excuse in the past few months as to why I missed school . . . including:

been sick,
been robbed,
been nearly run over,
been helping the sick,
been helping the robbed,
been helping the nearly run over.

Tessa, being a parent, does not back me up when it comes to good excuses. Mrs Barratt usually rings her in the evening, tiddle, tiddle, tiddle, 'Just thought I'd let you know' . . . da da, da da, da da.

I can imagine Mrs Barratt's side of the conversation, especially when Tessa replies, 'Yes, you're right, I don't think she was run over either. (pause) A robber? Oh really? Last week? Again?'

Tessa and Mrs Barratt always agree. It's sickening. My ideas and Tessa's hardly ever match any more. Sad. We used to be really good friends. She used to be on my side.

I was just thinking about this generation gap, kicking a few stones, keeping look-out for the dive-bombing magpie at the end of our street, sort of wandering along like every teenager does, when . . . I turned the corner and . . .

A police car is parked right outside our house. There is a posh car as well. I can't move. Panic wells up inside, takes hold, paralysing my whole body and my brain.

When I am in this state, not a thought can go through my head. I have no control. I would be sick if I could, I would scream if I could. But I can't.

From somewhere right at the back of my neck, I find my willpower. Stop it, stop it, cool it. Slowly the fear subsides, but the police car and the posh car remain.

They are for real. They are waiting for me.

So what?

5

As I near the house Tessa's sobbing gets louder. I step into the doorway. She stops crying, clasps her face like she has seen a ghost and scurries into her bedroom, moaning.

I see a man and a woman in police uniforms. Dr Jago, in his light brown suit, follows Tessa into the bedroom.

The policeman catches my arm and firmly steers me to the sofa.

'Sit down,' he says angrily, 'we've got a few little facts for you.' I sit heavily, banging the groceries. Tomatoes roll free.

'This is the last time we waste time looking for you, little lass,' he said. 'Where have you been?'

My mouth is sealed with super-glue.

He continues, 'Your mother is near a nervous breakdown with your truant behaviour. She doesn't deserve someone like you. Do you know what happens to kids who persist in runnin' away, shirkin' school, gettin' everyone frantic, wastin' valuable police hours? Do you? WELL DO YOU?'

The policewoman starts pulling his sleeve from behind.

'Leave her, Jim,' she mumbles.

Dr Jago is back, now he is moving towards me.

The lady cop continues, 'In the last three months or so, we have had so many false alarms about you, we've spent 17 police hours looking for you. That time could have been better spent helping to protect people who are really in trouble.'

The big one butts in, 'Children like you get put in special homes for everybody's peace of mind.'

At this moment our pokey neighbour, Mrs Angle, walks in. She is followed by her snivelling brats. The policewoman takes Mrs Angle to Tessa, to comfort her I guess. The brats stay and geek. It's a while since we had a police arrest in our street.

Dr Jago is leaning down. He takes my elbow and gently pulls me out of the sofa.

He says to the police, firmly, 'Thank you.' They get the message and leave without another word.

Then to me, he says, 'Let's go.'

His is the smart car—low, black, like something James Bond would drive. We zip away, in silence, and he burns along the highway to I don't know where.

We take a turn-off through big iron gates that open quite magically as we approach. The house they lead to is really something. I must be dreaming.

Dr Jago takes me through the front door and into a grand room. This certainly isn't a home for delinquents.

'Wanted you to see where I live. Take a seat. I only invite my friends here. What would you like to drink? Orange? Coca-Cola? Milk?'

'Coke,' I say.

He touches a cupboard and it becomes a bar with a fridge. As our drinks tinkle into fine glasses, he explains, 'I think we must talk before things go really wrong.'

He advances slowly towards me, cornering me. There is no way out. He hands me the drink and talks down to me.

'What is happening to you happens to a lot of people, and unless you give me a chance to explain the way you feel, you will suffer on and on needlessly,' he says.

'Now I know it doesn't seem fair that your friends took their lives so unnecessarily,' he continues. 'You know and I know they didn't need to do it. Nothing is that bad. But perhaps we can talk about it. Together, we might be able to see some reasons for what happened to them and what is happening to you now, and to your mum, and to their relatives.'

I feel as if he is pushing my mental resistance into a tight corner. He seems to be coming closer. Dr Jago is so determined.

'What you want to find out,' he says, 'is why they did it. I haven't got that answer. *You have.*'

I'm jammed, so tight. He's squeezing me. My brain will burst.

He says, 'Tell me about the boys, Benji and Joel.'

Then it happened. I scream and I scream. His

24

mention of the names Benji and Joel made me flip my lid. I have exploded. I shout, nothing in particular, just noise, endless noise. Noise comes out of not only my mouth but my hands, feet, ears, my head. Yes my whole head, and it amplifies the noise so that it is unbearably loud.

I fall on his floor. My strength goes. I cry a big puddle onto Dr Jago's carpet.

When I am aware of him again, he is sitting back in a lounge chair opposite reading a magazine ... about fishing!

I could kill him. The humiliation. I'm on the floor, just destroyed, and he's reading about fishing!

He did this to me. But I can't fight any more. He's kind of whipped me weak like the First Fleet guards used to do to the convicts. They often didn't know what their crimes were either.

'Like to wash your face, Flame?' he says.

I am too weak to fight. How did he know that? Benji and Joel gave me that nickname ... and it was private.

Too bad. Nothing is private any more.

I will go and wash my face, then I might start talking.

6

The bathroom had too many mirrors, even the bags under my red eyes were three-dimensional. And I felt just like I looked—horrible.

I rejoin Dr Jago and he is still reading that fishing magazine like cool, cool, nothing is happening sort of thing.

I'll give it to him. I start talking.

'Their parents came to see me after *the event*,' I blurt. 'Just knocked on the door and said to Tessa, "Is Flame in?" Well, she didn't know who Flame was, so she told them they were at the wrong house.

'Then they bawled, both of them. They told her they had been watching the house, and they knew I lived there. "The girl with the flame-red hair," they said, "she is the girl our boys loved. She is the reason they are dead."

'I think they always hated me, even though we had never met.

'Tessa was struck dumb by their dramatics. She just

walked back into the house with one hand gripping her mouth as if she was scared of the noises that might come out.

'Mr and Mrs Goldstein followed her into the kitchen where I was waiting. Why me, why me, *why me*? My thoughts were stuck like a broken record.

'Mr Goldstein spoke first. "We mean no harm, my dear, we just wanted to meet you. Such a little one." He shook his head with a puzzled expression. "Bless you." Then he slumped down on one of our little kitchen chairs and started sobbing.

'I was rigid. Nothing in me could move. Not even a thought.

'Then Mrs Goldstein rushed at me and started hitting me on the chest and shoulders like I was her wailing wall. She started shaking me.

' "You killed them, they died for you, you must be wicked." She said it about three times before she, too, crumpled in a kitchen chair and cried large, growly moans.'

Dr Jago has forgotten his magazine—he is now writing furiously on that once-empty pad.

I wait for him to say something. I must have given him something to think about, to psychoanalyse, itemise, tabularise, depersonalise and hypothesise about.

That's his job. I am waiting for his answer. Here it comes.

'What did you feel at the time, when Mrs Goldstein was letting go?'

I can't believe my ears. Whose side is he on? I won't reply.

He continues the inquisition. 'Were you angry with her for the way she felt towards you?'

I'm furious now. I say, 'What do you think? Have a guess. You are supposed to know why we do what we do, why human beings are such animals, why they have to get revenge, get someone—doesn't matter who—just so they can prove to themselves that what happened wasn't their fault.'

Dr Jago is staring at me. After a long pause, he says, 'You understand so much more than you realise. I want you to keep that anger up, throw it out. We'll get to the bottom of this. I don't mind if you feel aggressive towards me, because at times my job can only be done by making you defend your feelings.

'Now,' he goes on, 'what did Tessa do when you were being confronted by Mrs Goldstein?'

'Tessa was not part of the scene. She was there, but she did nothing to protect me. When I think back about that, she was so far in the background that I wasn't aware of her being there.

'You see,' I explain, 'Tessa doesn't know, really know, that I didn't do anything to cause Benji and Joel to . . . do what they did.

'But she knows for sure that *she* didn't do anything to deserve all the pointed fingers and accusing looks that she says she gets wherever she goes in town these days.

'I guess she suspects I might have done something

wicked, like Mrs Goldstein believes. And I might have.
I *must have.*'

I'm yelling. I can't stand this room any more. It's
so false. I'm heading for the front door. I can't open
it. I'm beating it—my fists will hurt this door.

Dr Jago grabs my arms, twists them behind my back,
holds me against all my strength. I'm grunting, kicking
backwards. I miss. My fists hurt. I'm crying. He's letting
go.

I can hear him saying, so nicely, 'You must take
one of these three times a day. They will help you
relax and calm that fighting feeling you are filled with.

'Come now, I'll drive you home. I want to show
you the most beautiful foal on the way. He's dapple
grey, born yesterday.'

7

Those tablets make it even harder to chew untoasted muesli. I just can't hurry. Everything is going slowly, except Tessa. She is buzzing like a bee, wiping down the clean, shiny benchtop again and again as she waits for me to finish.

She is taking me to school today, right to the front gate. If my friends see me arrive like that I will die.

Lifesaver will not see me today. Hope he's not counting on my sandwiches. Perhaps I'll pop down later just to check.

Tessa spends a lot of energy on everything she does. Just compare the way I am doing the car seat belt up and the way she does it. She pulls it right out, jerks it twice to see that it still works, then she jams it into the catch, bangs it, tugs it and tests it once more by leaning forward abruptly.

My way is just to slip one piece into the other. I feel so sleepy today. I won't be able to concentrate.

Thank goodness Tessa realises I am embarrassed

by her driving me to school. She stops before we get near the playground. I love her really.

The group I hang around with stop talking as I approach. Funny the way you get to thinking everyone is talking about you all the time.

'Interesting?' I say, sarcastically. They look caught out.

After a while, Josey tries to save the day. 'Deciding what to wear to Fat Head's party.'

'If you feel that rude about Peter Connelly why bother going to his party?' I spit out defensively.

'Didn't you get an invite?' asks the bitch Kate, my ex-best friend.

'I'm not interested in boys,' I state.

'Oh ho ho,' someone says in a sing-song voice. I couldn't catch which one it was. I wasn't looking at them at that moment.

In the meanest tone I said, 'Well I'm damn sure boys aren't interested in you lot . . . titless baldies.'

It wasn't kind, I know. And the truth is I would give anything to be flat as a board, a carpenter's dream. I was the first to need a bra in our class. In fact people are so pokey I think anyone here could tell you the date I first wore one and that it was size 32 B. (B stands for big.) Now I'm 34 C!

It was a bad start to the morning, but Mrs Barratt was terrific. She didn't ask me for a note explaining my absence. I think she knows too much. Just a pity she keeps ratting to Tessa so I get into trouble twice.

She called me out to her desk while the class were

doing some exercises and she tried to explain some of the work I had missed. She even said she would stay in the classroom over the lunch break in case there was anything I needed help with.

That was kind of her. I went back to my desk and fell asleep.

Naturally I didn't take the midday pill as Dr Jago had instructed. I'm a walking zombie as it is.

Now school is over for the day, I feel more awake. Kate is following me out the gate. She is trying to make up, I think. She offers me arvo tea downtown. She doesn't have to hurry home, 'cos no one is waiting for her. Her mother works.

And I won't be missed either. Tessa will be with Dr Jago till five and, boy, am I feeling hungry. I didn't eat my lunch. I was asleep in the sick room, and anyway I've got plans for those sandwiches.

Kate, I notice, is getting a few spots. Zits we call them, a name that comes from the sound they make when you pop them.

I've got freckles instead, millions of them, even on my toes!

Tessa says she had them when she was young and they went. That's another good thing that could happen to me one day in the future.

We look in the chemist shop for the best stuff for Kate's zits. Just as we start talking to the chemist, in a kind of whisper, in comes Fat Head and friends. Zapped. Spotted. How embarrassing. Forget it.

Down to the cafe we go. Kate orders double-chocolate milkshake, waffles with caramel sauce and icecream and cream. I may as well have the same. She's paying.

We talk. Just like before, before you know what. She says her mother is making her a party dress. I tell her I found my invite in my locker. Fat Head's party is next Saturday.

Then she asks, 'Sally, am I still your best friend? I've got to know where I stand. If you don't want me to be, I'll go with Michelle and Julie.'

Sure I want a best friend. It's something you've got to have. It makes you feel strong. Kate is a bit stupid sometimes, tries to be everybody's best friend. I accuse her of that and she says that her mother says that it is best to be friends with everybody.

That shows that Kate's mother must be stupid sometimes too. You can't be everybody's friend. We're in gangs. These gangs are for friendship, not for warfare like in the movies.

If you don't belong to a gang then you are kind of piggy-in-the-middle, a lonely place to be in the playground. Right now I need friends to stick up for me.

'Sure,' I say. 'But you have to stick up for me, believe me first.'

Kate umms, hesitantly. 'Umm, umm, can I ask you something? I didn't believe it when I heard it and I told them it wasn't true.' She sucks noisily at nothing-left in her milkshake container.

What's coming?

'Did you have a nervous breakdown?' she asks with a surprised expression.

'When?' I query.

'This week?' She is impatient.

'Yesterday, to be precise,' I snarl.

She is genuinely amazed. A long silence follows. She is dying to pry some more. I am tempted to shock her.

'And I'm now being treated by a mind-bender. I hope to be normal again some day.'

'Thanks, thanks for telling me,' she mutters. Now she can't wait to spread the news. More noisy sucking at nothing.

'What's he like, the psychological doctor? The one who drove you away from your house yesterday?' she asks.

You see, she knows everything. Word spreads like melted butter in our town. The only secret I really have is Lifesaver.

'The nutcracker, you mean?'

She tries a quick laugh but gets back to her point of interest. 'Must be interesting, being psychoed-analysed, I think that's what Mum said they did. Finding out why your thinking is twisted.'

'Yeah,' I reply. 'You should try it. Anyway, thanks for the nosh.'

'And Mum said it happened on the bigger boy's birthday. What a day to smash yourself to smithereens!'

I've finished with her, well and truly. I prepare to go. Still got the sandwiches. But Kate has not finished. She is suddenly fearful that she will not get what she is really paying for.

'They did it near the lighthouse, didn't they? The papers said so. And Mum said they were found wearing blindfolds. What did they use? Was it tea towels? Handkerchiefs?'

'How would I know?'

You little weasel. I stand up, defiant, shell-shocked.

'J-just one other thing, Sally,' Kate stumbles over her words. 'Being your best friend, I have to know the truth. Were you really with them when they did it?'

At that remark, a bulletproof shield drops between us. I had no protection from her poisonous probing, or the painful realisation that so many stories, so inaccurate, were so well circulated. A bitter feeling killed the sweet taste of caramel.

'Make the rest of the story up yourself,' I said, leaving, 'but remember, I didn't jump.'

8

'Thank you for telling me about Kate,' Dr Jago says, thoughtfully. 'She is very involved.'

A fat lot of help that answer is!

'What do I do about her?' I demand.

'What do you feel like doing about her?' he returns.

Honestly, I don't know why psychiatrists are credited with helping people. They are charlatans, frauds. And that is a subject I really know a bit about.

I tell Dr Jago, 'I think you mind-menders are a waste of money. You are supposed to help people stop worrying, straighten out twisted thinking. Well that is what Kate's mother says you are supposed to do. But you're making me muddled. You're a con.'

I am angry. Fortunately, Tessa is not paying for this *con*. The government is; taxpayers are. I am going to be brought to my senses in the interests of national health.

'This is medico benefits,' I tell him.

Dr Jago ignores the insults. He flips through some folders and says, 'Let's try this. It's fun. Now, as quickly as you can, give me the first word that comes into your head after I say each word. I bet you set a record.'

He explains the game so a four-year-old could understand. 'I say beetroot, you say red, or vegetable, or salad . . . the first word you think of.'

Then he says: summer   And I say: hot

towel	fold
school	Mrs Barratt
bike	boys
ribbon	hair
band	sock
thunder	lightning
boy	friends
hot	night
sing	tickets
clean	shoes
dirty	Lifesaver
work	hard
photograph	torn
fire	cook
picnic	black
friend	Kate
light	house
dark	light
feel	fingers
secret	share
tunnel	hide
blind	bat
flame	

He says it again. '*Flame.*'

'There is no Flame any more,' I tell him. 'I don't want to hear that word again. You put it in just to make me mad. MAD. That was their name for me; that was what I was to them. Now they are not here. There *is* no Flame. *Get it?*'

I have to move. I go to the window, look down. It is a long way down. It must have seemed a long way down from the top of that cliff near the lighthouse.

Dr Jago jabs me with his voice.

'Tell me how you met Benji and Joel? Was it at school?'

A tired sigh leaves my body. I think the last traces of resistance I had to Dr Jago went with that breath. I can't fight him any more. I'm an emotional marshmallow. So why care? I'll take the soft option. I tell him.

'I met Joel first. He was in the debating team representing the School for the Blind. I was on the Dominican Convent girls' team. Must be nearly two years ago now. I was thirteen and a bit, Benji fourteen, Joel fifteen.

'Our teams made it to the finals of the debating competition held each year between all the schools in the area. This final is held at night so kids and parents can watch. It's scary. While the judges add up the marks, the schools sing their school songs and give three cheers for their debating team.

'I was so nervous that night, I could not look at the audience while our supporters were barracking.

Tessa was there, and she has a habit of waving. So embarrassing.

'Then they announced we had won, 15 to 14. Joel had been good but his team-mates had been a bit wet, lucky for us. Tessa stood up, clapping her hands above her head. No one else was standing up. She was smiling. "Well done, girls," she called out.

'I can still see her now, the only one standing up, and she was the last to stop clapping. As she sat down, Joel growled loudly, "Hope the silly bitch gets blisters."

'Dr Jago,' I ask, 'wasn't that a nasty thing to say? Poor Tessa. I felt so bad.'

Dr Jago keeps writing. He's like Lifesaver, deaf to all questions. I am going to get his attention . . .

'There is something I have never admitted to anyone,' I say, casual-like. 'Not even to my cat Miaow,' I add.

Dr Jago is suddenly all ears. He looks up, eyebrows arched.

'Yes, yes,' he says expectantly.

And then I tell him, 'I tripped Joel up as he walked backstage. Just put my foot out and bang, he fell like a stone. He had asked for it, sort of, because of what he said about Tessa deserving blisters.

'Unfortunately he hit his head on the corner of a chair and blood started pouring down the side of his face. I was sorry straight away. It was awful. If he hadn't been blind I guess he would have missed the chair. When I did it I wasn't thinking about

39

his blindness. I just did it. It was revenge.

'I think back on that night, often. I can still see Joel lying there. He started talking. I thanked God he was alive, just in a little whisper to myself. Everyone was fussing, producing handkerchiefs galore, asking what happened. Someone was calling for ice. Another said, "Needs a couple of stitches." '

Dr Jago wants to hear more. 'Go on, go on,' he says, but I have stopped because I have just noticed the tape recorder going.

'Do you have to?' I say, as sarcastic as I can.

'What?' he says, oh so innocent.

'Get this on public record?' I point to the offending machine.

Dr Jago turns it off. 'Trust me. Every word we share here in this room is confidential. I must have some records of our discussions so that I can review our progress. Would you prefer I write or use this recorder? You seem to object to both.'

'Wouldn't you?' I sulk.

Dr Jago starts to pack up, puts his file away, tidies away his collection of pens and pencils. I know what this means. He is finished. But I am not. I have to finish . . . he should know . . .

'Then Benji appeared,' I hasten. Dr Jago stops packing up, concentrates on me again.

'It was the first time I set eyes on him. Benji and Joel look like brothers, so I guessed they were. Benji was bigger, but you could see he was younger. Both had black, black, curly hair. I notice hair colour because very few people are unlucky enough to have a bright orange flare on their head like I have.

'Benji seemed more upset than Joel about the fall. "What happened? What happened?" he kept asking, looking around at everyone. I was frozen. Couldn't tell them. No one knew what happened, and I think only a gladiator would have been silly enough to admit the truth. The crowds would have got me.

'So I just left backstage. I went down to find Tessa. She was still really happy. She congratulated me all the way home. She was so proud.

' "You are a great arguer," she was saying. "When you get going I think you could persuade a Catholic priest that there is no Hell. What a good time we could have on this earth if there was no place of punishment." '

Dr Jago is now very interested, but I am exhausted. I slump back into the chair.

'Tessa,' I explain wearily, 'is very religious. I was glad she didn't mind my arguments in the debate.'

Dr Jago leans forward. Has he one *more* question?

'What did you debate that night?' he asks.

My answer: 'Is there life after death?'

9

Sunday is God's day in our home. Nothing happens. In fact Tessa can sit down on a whole pile of ironing, saying the work will have to wait till Monday because this is God's day.

Ironing accumulates during the week on the sitting room sofa. Don't ask me why. It looks awful. Consequently, I would only think of asking a friend home on a Tuesday after Tessa has done the ironing on Monday night.

Most of Sunday morning is devoted to church. We get dressed in our best (her expression: certainly not mine) and off we go. I put my mind into overdrive; no, perhaps I mean auto-drive. Not being a driver, I get these motoring terms confused.

We arrive at the Catholic church early. The priest, Father John, is always cheery. Getting the crowds is like winning lotto in his business. He always says to Mum 'Dear Senora Teresa, lovely to see you.' He is another local Italian. She hands out hymn books and I have to help her. Not a job for two really.

Then we make our way up to the front pew, past everybody. We kneel for a bit to say a personal prayer. I once asked Tessa what I should say. 'Just open your conversation with God,' she replied.

So I tell Him about my week, confess a bit, complain a bit. If Tessa is still on her knees, I ask God to bless my friends. I name a few. Sometimes I say bless Dad, wherever he is.

I don't tell Tessa I say that. Prayers are private.

The important thing at this point in the proceedings is not to get up too quickly, because everyone in the rows behind will know you had nothing to say to God.

Another way to spend time on your knees is to wonder what certain people are saying in their personal prayers

This week I asked Him to do something about my 'best dress'. As he could easily see, it is too short, too tight across the boobs and totally unsuitable for Fat Head's party.

Kate is getting a new one. How do I?

No answer, of course. Lifesaver, Dr Jago and The Almighty have a lot in common. And the party won't be worth going to anyway.

Hours later, it seems, we all shuffle to the exit to be farewelled by Father John, ticked off for attendance, freshly blessed.

Tessa chats for a while. She has many friends there. I keep an eye on her, waiting for her to signal that she is ready to go home.

She now beckons. I hesitate. She beckons, agitated.

43

Mrs Connelly, Fat Head's mother, has been talking to Tessa for the last five minutes. Now they stand united, waiting for me.

Neither of them wanted to talk when I arrive. Then Mrs Connelly simpers, 'Lovely little dress you're wearing . . .' (She got the little right.) 'And we're looking forward to having you at Peter's party. You got the invitation?'

I nod. Tessa's face is flushed. She is wringing the handle of her handbag. Her words then stumble out and they stab.

'Mrs Connelly knows the Goldsteins. They want to talk to you.'

'Yes dear,' says Mrs Connelly. 'Old friends of our family. Neighbours too. We share a back fence. Lots of chats, you know, over the fence on washing day. (laughs) Nice lady. So sad now. She wants you to know that she didn't mean to hurt you. She has found something she wants to talk to you about. Will you come and see her? I'll arrange the meeting.'

I freak. I run and I run. Going nowhere. I am going so fast, the world is a blur. Down side streets, nearly run over, past the police station, down to the beach. I can hide in the crowd. Yes, I will hide in the crowd of bronzed bodies. I fall on the sand. Voices buzz above me. Leave me alone. I'm just sunbaking like everyone else. Damn this dress!

10

A sudden summer squall cleared the beach about an hour later. From nowhere the wind came, the clouds covered the sun. The bathing beauties flurried around collecting their creams, shaking sandy towels out over my lifeless body, going ooh-aah, screech, giggle, giggle, gallop . . . gone.

I lift my head, sand grains stay glued to my dried tear stains. The beach is mine. The waves are wild, spitting white foam like a demented animal.

I feel calm now. Little drops of rain tickle my arms— the warning signs for the blanket of deep-grey rain moving towards me across the water.

I don't mind. I wish it were acid rain which could dissolve this dress.

The wall of water falls on me. My hair cascades down my back as a watershed. The dress clings. I knew it would.

Though I can hardly see where I am going, I know my way. I tread carefully round the rocks to where Lifesaver sometimes sits.

And he is there. I see his carry-all trunk first and then his black boots sticking out from his rock shelter.

I crawl in too.

'Your feet are getting wet,' I say. 'And so is your trunk.'

He doesn't answer. I try again. 'Mind if I stay under here till this passes?'

Lifesaver looks at me. His eyes are farther away than usual. He says nothing. It is one of those days. Lifesaver is 'not home'.

11

Tessa was ironing when I got home just at dark. I had never seen her do housework on a Sunday before. In fact the sink is usually piled high with dishes by this time of the day.

But right now, the place is spick and span, and the only messy thing is Tessa herself. She looks like a used mop—grimy and wrung out. She keeps ironing with frenzied concentration as the wire-screen door announces my arrival.

'That dress of yours has had it,' she says without looking up. 'Mrs Connelly is a good dressmaker. She says she'll make you a new one in time for the party next Saturday.'

I can't believe what I'm hearing. I replay the words very slowly to myself . . . Mrs Connelly . . . the one who admired my dress outside church today . . . has offered to make me another dress . . . in time for her son's birthday party next Saturday, with fittings taking place this week in her house which backs on to the Goldsteins's house.

That sure smells. It's a rotten trick, a devious plot, a bitter-sweet concoction of revenge and reward.

I imagine the scene: me standing near-naked in Mrs Connelly's sewing-room, draped in net tulle like a fly caught in a web ... Surprise, surprise, enter Spider Goldstein!

'I like this dress, I *love* this dress,' I tell her.

Tessa looks up, eyes the dress which I had purposely torn in several places just half an hour before in an effort to render it totally unwearable.

I can't describe the look on Tessa's face, but I have to make up some excuse, quickly.

'Fat Head's party is fancy dress. You've got to go as a character in a book, and I'm going to be Heidi when she was poor.'

Tessa is incredulous, shakes her head so the message goes right into the brain, shrugs her shoulders, and goes on ironing.

I love Tessa. I wish I didn't cause her so much pain.

'Looks like it's God's will that we tidy up today,' I say, trying to be positive. 'I'll go and tidy my room and then the whole place will look terrific.'

My room is cosy and private; no one comes in here. We don't have a cleaning lady who comes to our house weekly like some of my friends, and I'm glad we don't. I would hate to have a stranger move my things around.

My secrets remain secrets and I always keep my door closed so even Tessa doesn't know what goes on in here.

I find this den exciting. It's my cave in a wild, wild world.

I wouldn't know where to start tidying up. Everything on my dresser top is essential; most of the ornaments are party presents from when I was little, and I'm going to have them even when I'm grown up. My husband will have to learn to like them.

I catch a glimpse of myself in the mirror. Husband? What a joke. Tessa is never going to get the money to straighten my teeth, so I'll only be attractive to someone who is similarly imperfect. And that will only happen when he finds that he is not attractive to the girls with perfect smiles.

I'll be someone's second choice.

My legs are good. But you can't get married in swimmers.

Joel once told me he knew my legs were good by the way I walk. And he knew the way I walked because he was always listening to footsteps. He said, 'I'm an expert on strides. You can tell a lot about a person by the way they put their foot down.'

That is such a funny thought. Now I sometimes close my eyes and 'watch' the people go by, just like Joel did. Wooden floors are the most revealing.

'Do you want dinner?' Tessa is calling. I don't feel hungry much. Food makes me sick. I'll get anorexia nervosa, Tessa says, and I will die.

Just right now I'm too busy to eat. I'm looking for that box of private things that was under the bed. I know I put it there. It's the best place because

49

not even the vacuum cleaner goes under there.

Shoes, old sneakers, a typewriter I'm supposed to be learning on, junk and more junk under here. But that box is not.

I look in every cupboard. I haven't seen it for months. I haven't looked for it for ages, not since Benji and Joel did what they did.

Panic, that awful uncontrollable terror, gets a hold of me. I start throwing things around the room, everything is flying—shoes, books, ornaments, the typewriter . . . Where's my treasure box? Where's my treasure box? Where's . . .

Tessa's voice makes a slight impression. She's talking about 'getting Dr Jago'. She's gone. My box of special things has gone. I collapse on the bed, the tensions release my tired muscles and I sob, little, whiny sobs.

Dr Jago's hands don't hesitate. They take my shoulders firmly and lead me to his car.

The magic gates to the driveway of his mansion are waiting for us. They open and close as though some obedient doormen were there.

Inside, Dr Jago offers me the same choice of drinks.

'Those tablets I asked you to take,' he says while he prepares the drinks, 'are not being taken.'

I don't have to reply because he knows the answer.

'If you disobey my instructions, I'll have to arrange stricter supervision,' he threatens.

What does that mean, I wonder? I can't ask.

He goes on, 'Until we release the pent-up anger

50

you harbour, quite understandably, you will be likely to experience these outbursts of uncontrolled emotion. That's natural. I expect that. But you must let me help. I won't waste my time on stubborn, ignorant patients. Are you going to cooperate?'

I take the drink he hands me. He's watching me like a hawk.

I give a little nod. It means a big yes.

12

Sounds in the night can be so real. I mostly hear steps, someone putting their feet down on our wooden floors. The steps start slowly and usually get faster and louder.

I put my pillow over my head when I first hear them. That way, I can't hear or be seen.

After a while I listen again. By this time it is hard to hear the steps because my heartbeat is so loud, but I know they are there. Extrasensory perception, Joel would say. So I jam the pillow back and press it hard so the only noises I have to live with are within my head.

I used to wake Tessa up to look for the intruder. She would stare at me for a while, unblinking, eyes wide like a corpse on TV. Then together we would sneak from room to room putting every light and radio on till our place was ablaze with light and sound from around 2 a.m. till dawn.

Afterwards, neither of us would sleep a wink and at breakfast I would be in trouble.

So now I tell her *after* I have had a bad night. I wish I didn't have to tell her, but being awake at night seems to be a long time in a person's life. It's important. Here goes.

'We had a visitor last night,' I say.

Tessa butters both sides of one slice of bread.

'Mmm . . . heh,' she replies, and puts the buttered slice in the toaster. She is coaxing the toaster to swallow it, but it is a very temperamental machine and hitting it on the side does not do the trick.

'That's supposed to be my lunch,' I point out.

She notices it is overbuttered and throws it out the kitchen window. We always throw stale bread out onto the lawn for the birds. That butter will be a surprise.

I continue, 'He came up the steps, down the hall, went round the sitting room and into the bathroom and, ages later, he left.'

Tessa stands rock still. She takes one of those big breaths and holds it. Slowly her hands begin to move, imperceptibly at first, then with determined strength they squeeze the sandwich loaf so that it is all one piece of dough again.

'Didn't you take your tablet last night?' she shouts.

'No.' I shout too. 'I can't think when I take those tablets. I live in a fog. I can't feel. How would you like that? There is so much I have to decide about. I have to decide about what I am going to tell Dr Jago. I can't do that if I'm asleep.'

'You are exaggerating,' she fights back. 'You know

53

I take those tablets too and I'm not gaga. Am I?'

I'm tempted to say he should increase the dosage.

Please stop shouting at me.

She goes on, 'You hear that intruder, as you call him, coming into our house almost every other night. How does he get in?'

Tessa rushes by. She is now in the hall. She has gone there to convince herself that I talk rubbish. I can hear her. I think the whole street can hear her.

'There are seven locks on this front door. I bought the lot, and not even Houdini could get in.'

Tessa is back in the kitchen doorway again.

'Your visitor must be a ghost. Seems like a harmless one. Doesn't hurt a fly. Doesn't steal a thing. From what you tell me, the only thing he does in this house is go to the loo. Forget him, I tell you. Forget him.'

Tessa stomps over to the sink bench. She moves like the proverbial cat on a hot tin roof. She is agitated. I make her like that. She was whistling when she started to make my school lunch, and now she is hopping mad.

Funny thing about Tessa though, she can change her mood so quickly, just like a projector shows another slide. Click! Another Tessa.

She picks up the poor sandwich loaf, turns it over for full appreciation of the damage she has wrought, laughs lightly with feigned surprise and chucks it to the birds.

Seems she has flipped her mood-slide, thank goodness.

'You'll have to order your lunch,' she says, carelessly, as she plucks her daily ration of tissues from the box. She takes out her small change purse, drops a two-dollar coin on the counter, then checks her face in the mirror attached to the lid of the little purse.

Tessa always pouts when she checks her face. So silly, because no one else sees her with that look. She is really shy. When she hands out the hymn books at church on Sundays, her chin stays close to her chest and she looks nothing like she does when she looks at herself in a mirror. Perhaps she is practising and one day she will front up to Father John, pout and say 'Hey there' in the hope that he will say 'Cool, baby, good to see you'.

Without looking at me, she leaves.

'Don't be late for school,' are her parting words.

The screen door bangs her goodbye. Her sharp footsteps fade.

I *will* go to school today. At lunchtime, I think. So much sorting out to be done urgently. Dr Jago now wants to see me every day.

Today I will take my evening tablet half an hour before my appointment, so he can see for himself how dumb I become.

Right now my room needs to be put together again after my turn—a fit of madness is a very messy thing.

Some of my precious ornaments did not survive. And the typewriter is now wonkier than ever. In fact, some keys have broken off completely. There used to be a few keys that didn't work, 'cos I can remember trying to type out that thing Benji and I did for Joel—it ended up looking like it was in code. Oh dear! But now, I would have to respell the English language to make this machine useful.

Best place for it is under the bed. I start shoving. It won't go.

I look. There is my treasure box. It has come back.

13

Everything was there in my treasure box. It had been moved around, but it was there. The diary, the hair ribbons, the ring made of silver foil with a Jaffa as a gem, the Star of David, the leftover marijuana joint, the book titled *The World of Psychic Phenomena*, the pebbles and the miniature lamp . . . (no kerosene left, which I guess explains the stains on the diary).

But how do I explain the disappearance and reappearance of the box?

Tessa must know. How could she do it? She is not supposed to come into my room. She says, 'That's your domain; live in it as you will.'

She's been lying. She's been spying.

I let her have her secrets. I saw her once, not long ago, walking arm in arm with a man. I didn't mention it 'cos I should have been at school.

What counts is that I didn't look purposely. She has. She has been touching all these things, maybe reading all these words.

The kerosene has really mucked up the diary, but

I can still work it out. Hope she couldn't. The code words should have thrown her.

I sit on the bed and stroke Miaow. She likes having her tummy scratched. She purrs. I open my diary, looking for the first meeting with Benji.

Here it is: October 14, now nineteen months ago. I didn't need code words then. This was three weeks after the debate. I'd been feeling bad about Joel's fall. I wanted to know how he was. I heard that he knew someone had tripped him, but he didn't know who. I was scared to ask about him in case I looked like the one who did it.

This is what I wrote:

Bit of luck today. I spotted Joel's brother in the town library. I was in a hurry to return some overdue books and race on to Kate's house. Then I saw him. A library is an easy place to look busy, so I grabbed the nearest book—*All You Need to Know About Desktop Publishing*—and tried to think.

He had a mate with him and I couldn't talk to both of them. Then Benji went behind a stack by himself and I walked right up to him. I just blurted it, 'How's your brother?' He seemed to know who I was straightaway. 'Fine,' he said, very friendly. Then he told me that Joel wanted to meet me. I got a fright when he said that 'cos I thought he must suspect me. I swung round to race off, but he said, 'No, come back. Joel thinks you're clever. He wants to meet you to continue the argument you started in the debate. He's kind of into that weirdo world.'

And I guess I wanted to meet him too, because of

what I did to him. I knew then I would never tell him that I tripped him, but I would make up for it somehow. I am kind, usually, and no one would want to have it on their conscience that they maimed a blind boy.

I remember asking Benji right there at the library how bad the cut over Joel's eye turned out to be.

He said, 'Hard to notice it on his face. His eyes are not his best feature anyway.' He smiled when he said that.

Benji wasn't really being cruel. I knew by the way he fussed over Joel that night when he fell that he loved him a lot.

The first time we all got together, all three of us, was at the Rotary Carnival held down at Commemorative Park. Benji said he would take Joel there and we would meet. Okay. That was fine.

I planned to have Kate with me, but when she found out we were meeting up with Benji and Joel, she went off saying, 'My mother will be disgusted to know you left me all on my own just to be with those boys.'

Ooowaah, she can make me mad.

Miaow climbs onto my chest. She likes my full attention whenever I lie down to read. She likes being talked to. She knows more about Benji and Joel than Tessa will ever know.

Yet Tessa thinks she knows all. She would often say to me, 'They are Jewish and we are Catholic and there is a big difference.'

'But,' I would remind her, 'you have only set eyes on them *once*.'

'It is not a difference you see with your eyes,' was her stock reply.

So, with her attitude being what it was, Miaow and I shared secrets—more and more secrets.

At the Carnival I wandered round on my own till I bumped into Benji and Joel. They were playing the chocolate wheel. They just nodded at me as I came to stand beside them. I felt spare.

They were having such fun. Joel was doing the spinning and Benji was doing the paying. They seemed determined to win a prize. People with nothing better to do were watching.

The scar on Joel's eyebrow was still covered with sticky plaster. But, like Benji said, it wasn't going to be the most disfiguring thing about him.

Benji was good-looking as soon as you saw him. He didn't have to 'grow on you'. That is an expression Tessa uses to describe plain people. Joel would have been good-looking except for his eyes—they were sunken.

When I first met Joel, face to face, I had to concentrate not to look at his eyes. Not that he would have known, of course, but they were so badly made by God that I would miss what he was saying if I looked at them.

He had a strange habit of screwing his eyelids up tight when in bright sunlight. Just like I do. I mentioned this to him one day and he asked, 'Are we both shying from the light?'

He talked in silly riddles sometimes. I was supposed to understand because he thought I was clever.

That day at the carnival had a moment I won't forget.

The wheel slowed to a laborious stop, tick . . . tick . . .

60

tick, and it landed on THE number—the winning number. It was red. Everyone cheered, and slapped Joel on the back.

The caller bent down low from the heights of his truck and asked for their names.

'Got to announce this, boys,' he said. 'What's yer names?'

'Benjamin and Joel,' they said.

'No surname? Dear, dear,' said the showman, and the crowd were with him.

'Goldstein,' said Joel, boldly.

'Ah, hah,' said the caller. Then in his loudest voice he told the world, 'Ladies and gentlemen, our ham has been won by none other than Masters Benjamin and Joel *Goldstein*.'

At the time I didn't know what was so awful about that. I just knew something was wrong. The mutterings told me that. Benji kind of snatched the ham with one hand and Joel with the other, and we pushed our way out of the crush of people.

They gave the ham to me because Jewish people don't eat ham. Well, the Goldsteins definitely don't. I had to take it home to Tessa. She asked me where I got the money to play chocolate wheels at fun fairs. 'I found it,' I said.

'What luck,' she said.

And so we ate ham, and only ham, for one month. Now, like Benji and Joel, I don't eat ham. How much of this will I tell Dr Jago?

14

Suddenly my watch says 1.30 p.m. Just like that—
1.30. No warning. *Hell* . . . oh Hell! The bell will be
ringing at school, the kids will be just metres from
their desks, but I am light years away. I'm still here
at home. Tessa will kill me.

I rush to the kitchen clock. It says the same. Where
did the time go? That phantom intruder must steal
time; perhaps he creeps in and changes all our time
machines.

There is just one more time-ticker in this house
which I can check. It is in Tessa's dresser, kind of
hidden in her underwear.

It was Dad's and it was still going last time I chanced
upon it. Kate and I were dressing up for a part in
our school play. I needed sexy underwear and Tessa
had said I could help myself. 'You can wear whatever
you find,' she said.

She had forgotten she was keeping the watch there,
out of my sight.

I put the watch on just for fun and some brief black

lace numbers and then walked out to show Tessa.

Kids don't think deeply about every little thing they do, but Tessa thinks that girls my age scheme the whole time. She jumps to crazy conclusions so quickly and I'm not ready for her.

When she saw that watch, she went wild.

'Take that off, immediately,' she said, racing at me with the kitchen knife, shaking it, a bit of onion still stuck to the end of it.

'How dare you, how dare you?' She yanked the watch off, twisting its expandable silver band till it snapped shut on her hand with a stinging ping.

She yelled in pain. 'Sometimes I know the devil is in you, so help me God. Why would you want to get to me by flaunting his watch?'

Kate joined us, attracted by the noise.

She said, 'Don't worry, Mrs O'Leary, it doesn't go with the gear anyway.'

That watch—now I'm looking for it again. He used to put a two-year battery in it and he only left fourteen months ago, so it should still be going.

Found it. It says 1.43 p.m. and I believe it. Too late to go to school. Nothing would be more noticeable than arriving at school at 2.15 p.m.

Could I blame the weather? I look outside where the rain is smacking our driveway and the chilly autumn wind is tormenting the trees.

Hell *is* on earth. What am I going to do? If only I could turn back the clock. I've heard that expression, but before this very moment I wouldn't have wanted

63

to. There haven't been that many wonderful times that I want to live again.

That is a cruel thing to say. Sorry, Tessa. You do try. I'm sorry. And I start to cry.

The telephone rings and I stop in mid-moan.

When it gives up, I breathe again. I've got to do something to conquer this fear. I'll have a sip of her sherry. Just a sip. That relaxes.

Yes, it does. Better than lunch. It actually feels like fuel all the way to my stomach. I won't need his silly pill to be a dill when I visit Dr Jago.

Bet Lifesaver could do with some of this warming liquid. He must be cold today, sheltering under his favourite rock ledge. But he says he doesn't drink— he can get to cuckoo land without alcohol. If it wasn't raining, I would like to go and see him. He is fun to talk to even when he doesn't answer.

Must set the alarm to be sure I leave this house in time for my appointment—rain, hail or shine. Dr Jago is going to listen to a few home truths about these sedative tablets he insists I obliterate my mind with.

Two hours till I front up. Time for a little radio maybe, a bit of beat, that's it. Nice and easy does it all the while.

I lean down and pull out the treasure box. I'll put this ribbon in my hair. That's better.

Should really light the little lantern. '*You light up my life*' are the words on the front of its heart-shaped glass base.

Just a little kerosene and it's away. Hey. Such a tiny flame. It makes me smile.

May as well light this joint too, get rid of it, as I'm sure Tessa knows it is here now. She'll be surprised. Next time she comes a-prowling and a-prying, it won't be here. What a laugh.

Drag. Drag. Smoke curls wave the air like the puffs of a genie's lantern. Mood magic.

15

Dr Jago's building looks so funny today. The red bricks look silly. They start me off on the giggles and when I get the giggles, I can't stop. Kate will tell you that.

Giggling by yourself is interesting to other people. Those waiting for the lift are fascinated. They stare. Perhaps they like the bow in my hair. I take a bow. They are goofs of the totally humourless kind.

So is Dr Jago's secretary. Prissy old duck. I swish past her. She is a joke.

'Wait, Miss O'Leary. Wait, Miss O'Leary,' I can hear her calling.

I don't care to wait. I'm on my way. I'm early. I'll surprise him. He'll say, 'Nice to see you're so punctual,' in his forever-so-soothing voice.

What a laugh. I can't stop this giggling.

Whooosh. I throw open his door. What I see takes a while to sink in. Getting the picture takes longer when you're stoned.

Dr Jago is by the window and someone is lying back in that manic chair, the one that tips people this way and that into positively demeaning positions.

He told me he had given the chair away, but he must just hide it for my visits. A comedy of manners. I giggle again. Joel was right, I am not a fool.

Dr Jago has raised his hand to the STOP position like a startled traffic cop. I get his message but I can't go back . . . the giggles are gurgling out of my throat like the sounds a kookaburra makes as it revs up for a big belly laugh.

Then it happens. I burst. Vomit spews forth with the velocity of a volcanic eruption, projecting mayhem.

The old secretary bag rushes in. She grabs my ponytail and the back of my dress. She is squealing, pulling me backwards out of the room. I hate her. When I catch my breath I'll . . . I'll . . .

Dr Jago comes at me from the front. I reach out to him. 'Hold me . . . HOLD ME,' I'm yelling.

I watch his tie coming closer, then going away. I fight. She pulls. I struggle. I win. He holds me. I cry.

Slowly the pressure in my head subsides. Dr Jago coaxes me out to the waiting room.

'Wash up a bit,' he says pointing to the ladies loo, 'and we'll go for a walk in the park.'

As I put my hand on the door to the loos, it opens. I step back and out comes that secretary, bucket and mop in hand.

She says everything she had to say to me by

scrunching her thin lips so that her face looks like a map of bad soil erosion.

I wash out my mouth, splash my face with cold water again and again, slap it like it deserves. It doesn't improve my looks, but they are beyond repair.

Dr Jago did not seem to mind, though. He takes my arm and, as we wait for the lift, he says, 'I've found some baby willy wagtails who are learning to fly. You'll love them.'

16

The fog in my head begins to clear as we walk to the Botanical Gardens. I begin to feel better. The Mintie Dr Jago gave me almost replaces the horrid taste of sick.

He holds my elbow as we cross the roads. If anyone noticed us they might think he was my dad.

I tell him that.

'Do I look much like him?' he asks.

'Nope.'

'Any similarities?'

I'm getting to know Dr Jago. I can pick it as soon as he gets hooked on a line of questioning.

'You want to know about Dad, don't you? What hang-ups I've got about him, don't you?' I say.

He nods. 'I'm interested,' he says, casually, as that is his style of interrogation.

I'll tell him. Who cares?

'Tessa is the one who has hang-ups about him, not me,' I insist, and I describe that scene with the watch and how she went off her brain.

We get to the tree where baby willy wagtails twitter and flutter in their tiny, immaculate nest. We sit on the grass nearby. Dr Jago explains that experimental flights take place about every half-hour. We must be patient.

'Where is your dad now?' Dr Jago asks.

'We don't know. Not a clue,' I tell him. 'Tessa says she doesn't want to know, and I'm sort of glad I don't because the police have asked me and I can honestly say that I don't know.

'I'd hate to get him in trouble. Could be somebody after him because he knows everything that happens at the racecourse and sometimes there are bad people working there.

'Dad is a really good bookie and really popular. I went to the racecourse with him many times and I would sit most of the day on the box he stands on to call out his prices.

'I was safe from the crowds there. The noise of everyone shouting is frightening.

' "You can bet on Frank O'Leary" was the sign above his stand and it seemed that people shouted the name O'Leary all day.

'He was very popular. "O'Leary sure has kissed the Blarney Stone," they'd say as he rattled on non-stop all day.

'And then near all night. After the races he would 'have a jar' with his track mates, and talk and talk. They would drink on and I would wait and wait in the van with the money.

'I opened the bag once and there was so much money. I was scared then. I didn't want to be robbed. I sometimes lay on the floor of the van so I couldn't be seen, and I swear if someone had come for the money I would have let them take it.'

A little willy wagtail launched his tiny frame, flapping his wings like fury. He's rising, falling, falling, plop. Just like Icarus.

We laugh. Dr Jago can be heard, but not seen, laughing because his moustache masks his teeth.

'Why did he leave you and Tessa?' he asks.

If only I knew.

'No idea. I've already told you that,' my voice firms.

'The last time you saw him, what happened?' Dr Jago persists.

'You're not unlike him, you know that?' I'm cross now. 'He used to badger Tessa when he came home drunk, badger and badger her, about where she had been, and why did she need frilly underwear and who did she wear it for and how many men had seen her in it . . . and on and on.

'Poor Tessa. Her goodness is never in question. She prays so much. She believes in Hell. She is so terrified of Hell and the confessional that she finds it hard to admit a parking fine.

'One Sunday Dad got up early, hangover and all, and stumbled out to get the paper. He was there to pick it up almost as the paperboy dropped it. I watched him through my bedroom window.

'He was looking for something, on the front pages

71

first, then on the back sports page. Whatever he was expecting must have been on the back page. He pulled it off and slipped it inside his pyjamas.

'The paper then had no front page. He stood for a while on the garden path, his mind wrestling with this problem. Then he trotted quickly over the road and dropped the rest of the paper into a council bin.

'When Tessa couldn't find the paper, Dad said the paperboy was hopeless. I said nothing.

'About an hour later, while Tessa and I were doing the muesli munch, he came out with a bag of clothes and his bookie's bag.

' "Got to go to a race meeting," he told us.

' "On a Sunday?" Tessa queried. Then he flew into her with words, accusing her of being dishonest, cheating him, being untrustworthy.

'And she was hitting him with her little fists saying, "You're for Hell, there will be no eternal salvation for you."

'And as he disappeared for good, Tessa screamed, "Now the Devil is saying you can bet on Frank O'Leary."

'The police came round looking for him later that morning. I heard just bits of the conversation—"wanted for questioning", some problems coming to light about "fixed races". I don't know what that means.

'What does it mean, Dr Jago? Fixing a race doesn't sound bad?'

Dr Jago lifts his hands. 'Look,' he said, and another amateur flyer hits an air pocket. Plop.

72

While we watch the poor little wretch trying to gather his wings and pull himself together, Dr Jago says, 'Do you feel let down by your dad?'

17

It is amazing Dr Jago did not ask me the recipe for that spew.

I would have told him ... take the last two centimetres of a bottle of pretty ordinary sherry and gulp them down, add one flat beer, a bowl of icecream and a marijuana cigarette, and you'll have a laugh you'll remember for a long time. *Disgusting.*

I'm so, so glad he didn't ask me to explain exactly what I had been up to. I suspect he knew some of the ingredients. He's not stupid. But he let me be. I can't for the life of me figure out why he didn't even mention it. He would have his reasons.

Ooowaah, Dr Jago's floor! I can see it more clearly now than when it happened yesterday. And that silly bitch tugging at me like a terrier dog, trying to protect her master and his patient from an unscheduled, chundering child.

Come to think of it, the surprise of it all was probably very good therapy for that misfit in the crazy chair—I could see that his only worry after I burst into the room was how he was going to get out!

I'm lucky Dr Jago didn't launch into a spiel about corrective therapy for drug use. I've enough punishment to cope with—that joint I smoked is now a broken promise I made to Joel and I will have to live with that for the rest of my life.

I am ashamed. I'm sorry Joel. It's harder being strong-minded since you left.

I have decided to search back through this diary early every morning to work out what I will, and what I definitely will not, tell Dr Jago.

He does *not* need to know about the day I got drugged at Rosehill Racecourse, that's for sure. Oh boy. That was bad.

Here is the entry in my diary—Anzac Day, April 25. I wrote:

Tessa worked at the church today making things for the fete. I persuaded Benji and Joel to go with me to Rosehill for this mid-week race meeting. Told them what fun horse races are: the excitement, colour, challenge . . . you know, all the hype of the TV advertisements.

They agreed to give it a go, but Kate wouldn't come with us because her mother says all the worst types in town gather at race meetings. I told her she was insulting my background. She said she didn't mean to. I wonder if Kate could go for one whole week without putting her foot in it.

I was hoping I might see Dad again. He's been gone a few months now and we've heard nothing. I know we don't want to after what he said to Tessa but I would just like to ask him what 'fixed races' are. He is good at explaining the business. I guess he would have told me the meaning at some time but I have forgotten now.

All the way out in the train, I imagined seeing him, standing high on a box, shouting, 'Your bet's safe with O'Leary, best bet around.'

I told Benji and Joel that we would hear my dad as soon as we stepped on the course.

We looked and looked for him. I asked some familiar faces if they had seen my dad or knew where he was. 'He's full of baloney, little one,' an old bookie warned. 'You and yer mum are better off without him.'

At one point I lost Joel and Benji. They went to find the men's, and then Benji couldn't remember where they left me waiting. Being blind, Joel was no help. He tags along, being bumped into. He should wear a flashing light on his head, like an ambulance, so that people would clear out of his way.

While Benji and Joel were gone, I was befriended by some guys. They were nice, trying to cheer me up, offered me some smokes. Soon I was as high as a kite; as silly as a rabbit. These guys decided to take me with them. Suddenly I felt frightened. They were taking me towards the car park. Then I saw Benji. I was so happy to see him, I just cried.

Joel was cross with me, I could tell. But Benji wasn't. He put his arm around me and supported me all the way to the station. I hung around his neck like a rag doll. It was comfy. People thought we were young lovers.

Joel would like to have walked away from us but, as always, he had to hold on to Benji's elbow.

They delivered me home. Tessa met us. Oh dear. They told her I had eaten something rotten, but Tessa was of a mind not to believe anything *they* said.

Tessa had particular questions she wanted answered and from that day I knew I was going to have to keep some secrets just to keep her happy. I've got to have some fun.

Miaow is scratching at my door. She wants her daily rub. Come on in; up you hop.

Joel also had a lot to say about that excursion. Whenever we met, for weeks afterwards, he would lecture me as if he were my keeper.

He went on and on about how I was a perfect cut-out of a junkie: gullible, weak-minded, emotional and showing all the signs of falling into the trap of trying just a little, believing I was smart enough to get out of it.

He warned me not to try another drug. 'No smokes, no tablets of any kind, and no shoot-ups for God's sake. You'll lose control of your mind, then of your body. And, of all people, I don't want that to happen to you,' he said.

One afternoon after school, I met Joel tapping his way along the street. We chatted and he suggested we find a quiet place to talk. I took him to a bus stop shelter not far away.

He produced a joint and held it high near my face.

'See this,' he said, 'I went to a lot of trouble to get this. It's mine, but I want you to mind it for me. You know what I think about drugs, and so you know what I'll think about you if you smoke it.'

He was quite bossy. Like he owned me. He was

waiting for me to give him my reply, to promise.

'Give us a break, Joel. You are making a big deal out of nothing,' I said defensively. 'Forget it. You've got the wrong picture.'

Damn it, I can be clumsy with words.

His head dropped. I felt sorry for him not being able to look me in the eye and bawl me out. He looked vulnerable. I took the smoke from him and put it in my pencil case. Perhaps I should have been glad he was worried for me.

'But thanks, Joel,' I said. 'I get your message. I'll keep it as a memento to bad habits.' I patted his arm. My hand can be kinder than my voice. 'And I sure do appreciate the lies you had to tell Tessa. I didn't want to tell her we had been looking for my dad. She says he is not worth looking for after what he has done. But he is still my only dad.'

I was just going to ask him where Benji was, 'cos I was beginning to think about Benji a lot, sort of romantic thoughts, just as I was going to sleep, when Joel surprised me.

'Can I touch your face?' he asked.

Then I really wished Benji were there. He knew how to make things seem like fun when Joel got serious. He would wink at me and then play a little joke with Joel and then we could all be relaxed. Benji wanted to do things with just me, I could read it in the way he looked at me sometimes.

But Joel had to be around. Mrs Goldstein told Benji,

'Always include your blind brother—he's missed out on enough already.'

I thought of that as I noticed Joel's hand searching for my face. I looked around to be sure no one was looking.

'Okay,' I agreed. Helen Keller always had to feel to see. Joel's hand came towards my face. I put it on my cheek.

His fingers touched so lightly, like feathers. Slowly they moved over my face, around my hair, and down my arms to my fingertips.

His feeling sense was so finely tuned that I knew I was taking shape in his mind. I was being recorded for all time. I shut my eyes, out of respect for his blindness, I think.

Or was it because I wanted to imagine I was alone with Benji?

Then he said, so softly, so sincerely, 'You look wonderful,' and I hated myself for cheating on him.

18

After that Anzac Day race meeting, every name in this diary is coded. Benji is Bev and Joel is Jill. But Kate can only be Kate—no one will ever change her.

The following day, Benji rang to see how I was. I have told him not to ring at times when I'm busy.

'Busy' means when Tessa is home.

I said very little on the phone, so Benji got the picture that I was 'busy' and we both hung up.

I turned round and there was Tessa, head craned forward like a person hard of hearing.

'Don't you know it's manners to say "hello, so-and-so", and then "goodbye so-and-so?" '

I replied, 'They know who they are.'

Well, she went right off. She ranted, 'I know who it was, I do, I do. It was one of those boys, and you are not doing yourself a favour by encouraging them. What if Father John sees you? There are plenty of nice young boys in our church group, and you don't give them a chance. You just ignore them. I talk to people after Mass, get to know them. It's the right thing to do. You just wander off as if you are a deaf-mute with nothing in common with them.'

I have never been able to talk to Tessa when she becomes electrified. I left, and she shouted after me, 'That's it, walk out on me. You're just like your father.'

That made me run, and I headed down to Lifesaver for a bit of peace and quiet. He has always been around.

I also had to find him yesterday because Tessa was cyclonic. Stupid Kate had called in and asked me, in front of Tessa, if the races were at Rosehill or Randwick on Saturday. Her stupid mother knows someone who has a horse running and they might go to watch it.

Well, Tessa said, 'We don't follow the races any more.'

And Kate said, 'Aw, but Sally usually knows?' Isn't that subnormal?

Lifesaver agreed it was. Well, he didn't say so, but he didn't contradict me either.

19

Now Tessa has a nervous rash. It is creeping along one side of her body—a fiery itch that inflames every nerve ending along the way.

I ring our local GP and tell him he has to hurry. He is taking an age. Oh, poor Tessa. She doesn't want breakfast. She is too sick. I'm not hungry either. I can hear her moaning.

Here he comes. I'm still in my pyjamas! I forgot to change. It doesn't matter with doctors. Sick people are always in their pyjamas.

I take him to Tessa and then listen just outside the door. He gives her the once-over.

'Lift up your nightie, mmhh, mmmhh. Other side. Lift your arm a bit for me. Sore? Open wide now, mmmhhhh.'

Having got the whole picture, he then starts the big inquest into every detail of her life.

'Eaten anything different in the last couple of days? Worn any different fibres close to your skin? Suffering any undue stress at the moment?'

I am all ears. She is going to complain about me.

Click, the bedroom door is closed (by the quack, I think) and I can hear no more.

I think doctors like him make house calls last and last so they can charge more. He will call this a 'long consultation', and it's the biggest bill.

I wait in the kitchen. I know his kind. Greedy and gossipy.

Dr Patterson comes to report just as I whack the toaster. I give him a matter-of-fact reception.

'Well, how is she?' I ask, sounding grown up.

'Not good? How are we going to manage?' He seems to be asking questions.

I can ask questions too. 'What's the disease?'

'Shingles,' Dr Patterson explains. 'It is a very unpleasant experience and your mother will not be well for some weeks. I'll be prescribing some medicine which will relieve the discomfort, but time will be the healer and she must be kept cool, calm and rested.

'Shingles is a relative of the chicken pox virus, not really infectious, but, as she is likely to feel pretty off-colour, I'd like to put her into hospital for the next few days. Have you a best friend you could stay with?'

'Yes,' I kind of squeak. I must not cry. 'When's Tessa going?'

Dr Patterson is writing something down. 'I'll have an ambulance call for her soon. Just because she is going in an ambulance, don't worry. It's the most efficient way to travel and she'll be in comfort all the way.'

83

I am juggling the hot toast: no plate to put it on. It drops on the floor.

He hands me the piece of paper. 'Ring this number this evening and they will tell you how she is getting along. This is the address. Perhaps you can visit on the weekend?'

And he goes, so suddenly, leaving me to look after Tessa, and myself. I'm so frightened.

I run to Tessa. I hold back the tears all the way along the corridor, but they get out as I enter Tessa's room.

She looks so awful, so ugly. Her face is blotchy and her skin everywhere seems angry. She is so distracted with the maddening fire in her skin that she hardly notices me.

I fall on her bed and she rubs my hair.

'Just a few days till they control the itch and then I'll be back. I've got a surprise for you, up in that cupboard. Get it out. Come on, get it out.'

She points to the cupboard and then closes her eyes to cope with her pain.

I open the door and there is a package, beautifully wrapped with green bows. I take it out, puzzled.

'Open, open it,' she urges from her sick bed.   Bow by bow it unfolds, tissue by tissue, a tip of lace, a peep of blue, a splash of colour . . . a pretty dress!

'Oh Tessa,' is all I can say at first glance.

'For the party,' she moans.

'Fat Head's party?' I repeat, incredulous.

'Try it on. Go on, go on,' she pleads, weakly.

I go into my room. I can't believe it. Very pretty with little yellow flowers and sleeves edged in white lace.

But for Fat Head's party, oh no! It's not fancy dress like I told her and she must have found out I was lying, but it is also not this kind of fancy dress.

This must have cost the same as straight teeth.

I hear wheels in our drive. It's the ambulance. I must get this dress on for Tessa, quick, quick. He's knocking.

'I'm coming, I'm coming,' I shout as I struggle in through the bodice without enough buttons undone.

'I'm here,' I say as I pull back the door. The ambulance officers are in white and they stand either end of the stretcher. How many times have I seen that scene on TV? But I never thought I would see it in my house.

I'm speechless. I wave towards Tessa's room.

'Ready for a bit of fun?' says the leader as he shuffles by me. 'You look swell in that dress.'

I bite my lip. I stand at the bedroom door as Tessa asks the officer to take two clean nighties from her drawer, her slippers and dressing gown. These few things are placed on top of her on the trolley and out she goes.

Her eyes roll over me as she passes. She smiles approval.

Cheerily, one of the officers says to Tessa, 'Mark my words, that little girl's going to set some hearts on fire.'

20

Interfering Mrs Angle is knocking at the back door. I saw her duck under the broken palings. That fence is supposed to be the dividing line between our lives and their lives, but she behaves as if it isn't there.

In fact, I wouldn't be surprised if she smashed those palings purposely, because they are the only three missing in the whole fence and the gap is in line with the shortest distance between her back door and our back door.

I'm trying to get my dress off, quickly, quickly.

More little knocks, the friendly, I'm-here, how-are-you? is-the-kettle-on? kind.

'Oooo-who! Ooo-who!' she is singing as she tiptoes through the kitchen. I meet her in the corridor. She has come over in a hurry, still has her full apron on and seems to be drying her dishwashing hands on it.

'Yer mum, dear, what's the matter?'

I'm in charge here. I am. I must not give her a good story to spread.

'She has gone for a check-up. Only went in the ambulance for the fun of it. Her brother is an ambulance driver and she had never had a go.'

'She never told me that. A brother as an ambulance driver? Thought she only had one brother? The one that, um, that is . . . um a cripple?' she pries.

Remembering my drama teacher's words ('Whatever happens, the show must go on') I say, 'Yes, that's right, but he drives an automatic. He doesn't need legs.'

Mrs Angle is absorbing all that. Her hands are still drying themselves. The apron is so dirty, she will have to wash her hands again when she has finished drying them.

Two of her brats join us. One of them has a very runny nose. Enough to make you puke. Mrs Angle wipes the snot off with her apron. Errrrruggghh!

'Want to come and stay with us while she's away?' she offers.

'No, thanks, I'm going to stay with my best friend, Kate. She's expecting me.'

Mrs Angle is peering over my shoulder into my room. I'm not tall enough to stop her. Her probing eyes and her probing mind are hectically busy.

'Been trying on the dress, have you?' she asks. 'Lovely isn't it? Yer mother was going to give you that surprise on Saturday morning, just in time for the party. But you got it early?'

Mrs Angle thinks a little more. 'Yer Mum not coming back before Saturday? This being Thursday?'

I find a reply. 'Depends how much checking they've got to do.'

I'm fighting, not just with her, but with the panic that wells up when someone corners me, probes, wants to dig inside for answers that hurt. I don't know how long I can hold back the scream. I take a deep breath . . . hold it.

'Ah well, you know we're there, just right next door, if there is anything we can do. We'll feed Miaow while you're gone. Better let you get to school, I don't want to be responsible for yer bein' reported missin' again. Toodle-oo.'

Bang goes the back screen door.

Bang goes my balloon of angry feelings. I let them out, let them pound themselves to death on my tear-damp pillow.

They get muffled, strangled, suffocated.

21

The wind likes fighting with my hair, so when I walk on the beach I take the rubber bands out and let the two of them battle it out.

On a rough day like today, my hair and the wind really have fun. My hair goes wild, it whips the air and lashes back at the tugging, tearing gusts.

It flicks my face and stings my eyes and twists and turns and knots itself into a tangle that will tease my hairbrush interminably.

This beach is the best place to be if I want to clear my head. It felt so thick and soggy after that bout of bawling but now, running against this wind, I don't care about the things that made me cry.

I'm as carefree as Lifesaver and, just like him, I'm carrying my worldly goods with me.

I'll go to Kate's house after school and somehow I have to warn Dr Jago I won't be visiting while I'm staying with her. Imagine saying, 'Kate, I'll be late home today because I've got to see my nutcracker.'

I'm going to see Lifesaver. I've got lots to tell him

and I've lunch for all the seagulls in Sydney. No point in leaving all this bread to our backyard birds.

The first sign that Lifesaver is 'at home' on his rock ledge is the gull activity just above where I reckon he should be. They are whirring and shrieking.

I pick my way around the rocks the only way I know to get there. He must go another way because he gets his trunk there, and that would be impossible to do on my route. I must ask him about that.

Yes. There he is. His shabby shape is a welcome sight. I haven't been able to see him as much as I would have liked to lately, because Tessa has told all the neighbourhood that 'since the tragedy, I have to be carefully watched'. She's frightened I'm going to do it too.

So I can't visit him when I think I am being followed. After all, he is my private, personal friend, and I think he wants things to stay that way.

He has added to his outfit a red hard hat, probably found on a building construction site.

'Hello, Lifesaver,' I say. 'I'm so pleased to see you. When I saw all the seagulls I knew you must be here, conducting their concert.'

He laughs, that really mad laugh of his—cascades of high-pitched notes finishing with a grunt. I can see he is in a talking mood.

'Come to live with me, have you?' he asks, nodding at my two overnight bags.

'Nope, going to live at Kate's house for a few days,' I tell him. 'I'd like to stay with you though.'

90

Lifesaver must know that the town gossips. He says, 'That would really get the tongues a-wagging.' He gives that loony laugh again.

'Get you locked up too. Anyone who thinks I'm sane has to be insane. Get it?'

'No, not quite,' I admit.

He explains, 'They would think you were insane, nuts, bonkers. Get it? Truth is no one knows where to draw the line between the sane and the insane. I know exactly where that line is, but they wouldn't listen to me, of course.'

I'm fascinated. 'Tell me, tell me where it is?' I encourage.

He thinks for a while. One-leg One, his pet seagull, lands on his hard hat and poops. Seagulls always do that unattractive thing just after they land. They could do it on their way here over the big blue sea, but no, they seem to wait. Uuuggghh.

'I cross that line,' he goes on, 'all the time, sometimes twice a day. It's as clear to me as a pedestrian crossing is to you.'

I want to ask him another question, but I can't think of what to ask. Quick, quick, he might cross the line and not be here.

'Lifesaver, um, um, do you know when you are in the mad world that you are in the mad world?' I dare to ask.

'Yes, yes. I'm in control. Like I told you before, I'm the director of all the actors who come into my head for rehearsal time. I tell them where to stand, how to improve the projection of their voices, the elocution of their parts, the drama of their gestures. And they are improving.'

He nods with satisfaction and puts his hands together. His hands are so dirty he'll get lots of germs when he eats my sandwiches.

I get the sandwiches out. I give him his share and start on mine. Talking to Lifesaver is tiring. I need brain food, and time to think.

The hard thing is knowing what questions I want to ask. Talking about other worlds and different levels of consciousness is very confusing. I had these times with Joel.

Eventually I sort something out. I ask, 'Do your actors come in from the spirit world? Like are they kind of voices that once belonged to somebody? You know, a person that died?'

After some time, he replies. 'I guess so. Migrating souls, I suppose. Restless sorts of beings, who stay with me half an hour, half a day maybe, and then off. Back to their supernatural world.'

I felt silly saying it, but then he is not frightened of madness. So I ask, 'Could they take a message back for me?'

22

Something I was really looking forward to seeing was the dress Kate's mother was making for Fat Head's party. Kate kept it hidden from me from Thursday night, when I landed on their doorstep, till Saturday morning.

So much stupid secrecy—you would think it was a bridal gown.

And now I have seen it, it is really not much. Nice? Yes. Different? Yes. Trendy? Yes.

But not FAN-TAS-TIC, like she said.

It must have taken her mother a lot of time to make. Not that that means a lot. Tessa says that simplicity is style.

Kate's thing is made with two colours, turquoise and black. It is in one piece, but the skirt part is culottes which are kind of gathered at the knees.

Her initials are embroidered just where one boob will be. How embarrassing. Kate hasn't got much so I suppose she hasn't thought of that. KC—her mother must be a dag to do that.

I wouldn't want SO'L emblazoned on my front. For one thing I might want to be incognito. Like when some jerk comes up at a party, I might want to say my name is Kate Conway. I just couldn't if I had SO'L staring at him.

The bottom part of Kate's new thing is the clever bit. The pants are in sort of stripes of black and turquoise, and, being pants, they have a casual, not-too-fancy look about them.

I feel it is embarrassing to go to a party looking as if you have tried to look pretty—like you're trying to attract the boys.

The cool trick is to front up looking as if you don't care too much if no one takes any notice of you. Then when they don't, you can say to yourself, 'Just wait till I dress up!'

Unfortunately, I can't strike that pose this evening because I'm putting on my new dress.

It's pretty yes, Tessa, it's so pretty, thank you, and I'll wear it proudly. When I rang tonight that doctor gave the meanest info on you . . . 'She is improving.' Well, if not, there must be something very wrong with that place.

Hope they take me to the hospital tomorrow to see Tessa. That will be after I have lived through the party, and Mass. Tessa will be pleased if I do her job and hand out the hymn books, all by myself.

23

We arrive early at Fat Head's place. If I hadn't been staying with Kate, I wouldn't be here. I wasn't going to come. No way.

There was a time when I used to invite myself to stay with Kate so we could meet Benji and Joel, but the fun has gone now, and Benji and Joel won't be at this year's party.

Mrs Connelly is clucky like a hen, not used to having girls in the house, says we're quite different to Peter (that's what she calls him) and her elder son, Mark. *I hope so!*

Mrs Connelly likes both our 'outfits', as she calls them, and tries to get the boys to say so too. *Embarrassing!*

This party can't end too soon. And I hope Fat Head doesn't unwrap the presents in front of everyone. My thing is so small. Presents always seem good enough in the shop but, as you hand them across to someone, you know you would feel bigger if the present was bigger.

I have given him a set of coloured pencils. I said to myself in the shop, 'These will be useful because we always need coloured pencils for projects.' Now they seem like a present for a preschooler, and Fat Head is fifteen today.

Everyone has agreed to try and call Fat Head 'Peter' while we are at his house.

Most people have arrived now and we're doing nothing, just looking bored. It is important to look bored at the beginning.

Mrs Connelly has by far the loudest voice in the room. 'Chips, anyone? Come along, move over here, what about something nice to drink? Peter will take charge of that, I'm sure.' Tut, tut, tut, she clucks. I hope she doesn't come near me.

Suddenly the music drowns her out. Heck. Who's doing it? Such show-offs. Trust them. So wet. These decibels will reach the police station without the neighbours having to complain by telephone. Like they did last time.

It was a good party last year. It started like this, I suppose, but soon it was fun. I wore jeans last year. Didn't have a party dress then, only my Sunday thing, and I got Tessa to agree it was too daggy.

Benji and Joel arrived late last year. They were older than Fat Head (Benji by one year, as he was fifteen then; Joel by two), but they were invited because they were next-door neighbours.

I was so pleased to see them walk in. Mrs Connelly marched them around the perimeter of the room, where we were all sitting, and she introduced them to us, one by one.

I said 'Hello' just as if I were meeting them for the first time.

It was perfectly obvious that Joel was blind, but Mrs Connelly had to say it. 'Now, I want you to be aware of Joel. He can't get out of your way as easily as you can get out of his.'

She meant well saying it, but he would have hated that. She was lucky he didn't give her an earful. He was inclined to do that to people who drew attention to his blindness, especially if they insinuated that blindness was an unfortunate handicap.

Joel believed he had made it an advantage—it had made him refine other senses, develop extra powers of perception and intuition.

He thought that at the end of the day he had a clearer picture than most people with useful eyes.

When Mrs Connelly had finished with him, Joel came straight back to me. We all moved along on the sofa and he sat beside me.

That's when he told me that insight was more important than sight.

'You can see much further if you can train your mind to reach into higher planes of cosmic consciousness,' he said. 'These people here are so earthbound that they are missing out on the pleasures of true harmony with the universe.'

I found that impossible to comprehend. And at a time like that it was impossible to concentrate—I was distracted by seeing silly Kate trying to flirt (she wouldn't know how) with Benji. She didn't have a hope. He looked so mmmmm, so hunky, chunky, spunky, and he was being funny with the guitar over on the other side of the room.

I couldn't take my eyes off Benji. Joel's voice was a whisper, or wasn't I listening? I wanted to be over where the fun was.

Everyone was laughing around Benji. Thank goodness, Joel couldn't see I wasn't looking at him. I hope he couldn't sense it. I kept saying 'yes' while he chatted.

Then I got impatient.

'This is not the place to talk about complicated life-and-death issues,' I told him.

But he went on, saying he would like to help me educate my mind and my soul, to help me open the door to spiritual experiences. Why me? He knew the way I thought.

'You know what I think about that sort of thing,' I said, 'all hoo-doo and hullaballoo. Don't you remember I said that in the debate, and my team won?'

Of course he remembered. Perhaps that was why it was still a challenge to convince me of the existence of a supernatural world? Or perhaps, I thought at the time, he was trying to convince himself that the mysterious world he argued for actually exists?

I stood up, but Joel held my wrist firmly. 'Another time, another time,' I said, brushing him off. 'I've got to get a drink.'

Then I didn't see him again for a while. I can only remember Benji and the good time we had.

We 'found each other', sort of, when we were playing chasings outside. It wasn't a proper game, just people started to chase, and get caught, and it was fun.

Benji caught me with a below-knee tackle. Thank goodness I had my jeans on, 'cos in a game like that your skirt could end up anywhere.

I felt a bit winded—first time I've been downed like that. But I wasn't cross. He held me tight and counted loudly to ten. I was sorry when he got there.

I wasn't in a hurry to get rid of him. All the other girls thought that he was dishy too, so I wouldn't have been too ashamed if Kate had seen him holding onto me and doing all that counting.

'What did you count to ten for?' I asked. 'That's for boxing.'

'Just felt like it. Any objections?' he asked.

'Not really,' I replied, nervously.

'What were you talking to Joel about?' he asked. He sounded just a teeny bit jealous.

'Oh nothing,' I told him. Joel's obsession is not exactly a winning party trick.

'It looked like more than nothing to him,' Benji insisted.

'Oh,' I said, beaten, 'he was on about his spirit world.'

Benji just shook his head.

'You started that,' he said, 'with that dumb debate last year. Since then he's been getting me to read all this New Age literature to him. Such a lot of mumbo-jumbo. *Real shit.* Scary too. I suggest you have another little talk to him. You might have won that debate, but you sure didn't convince him.'

I agreed. 'Creepy, isn't it? We'll have to think of something to put Joel right off that nonsense. Make him see it for what it is. It's crazy. We've got to bring him down to earth.'

'Yeah,' said Benji, 'Good thinking. Any suggestions?'

At that moment, Mrs Connelly came out, took one frightened look at all the exhausted bodies lying around on the lawn, including Benji and me, and said, urgently, 'Come inside, come inside all of you, immediately. We're going to play something Joel can join in, Blind Man's Buff.'

24

'Why are you telling me about this blindfold game at the party if you didn't stay around to play?' Dr Jago asks, without looking up from the notes he was scribbling.

'Because I've got to tell you something; I can't just sit here in silence all day,' I tell him.

He reminds me, 'Our meetings are only one hour.'

I hate the way he sticks to details all the time. He is as dull as a disconnected battery—no sparks of spontaneity, just predictably dull and dreary and boring . . . like this room.

I point this out. 'Half a minute in this room, with you, can seem like a whole day.'

Dr Jago keeps writing. Criticism about this sterile situation cannot get through a skin as thick as his. He is hardly human, just a body without emotions.

I give him the plain facts as I see them, because they affect me; they affect the way I feel about being here, the way I feel about telling private things to this dickhead. He is so inhuman, so unfeeling.

'Take a look at this place, just take a look. Stop writing, just take a look,' I demand.

Dr Jago looks around the ceiling, bewildered and as speechless as Alice in Wonderland.

I have to tell him what he is looking at. 'There is nothing of interest in this room. The walls stay the same yukky colour, the hounds in that picture will never catch the fox, you wear the same boring suit *always*, and of course that plastic plant in the waiting room doesn't change one leaf. *Nothing changes around here.*'

Dr Jago looks back at his pad, at what he has written, but his pen does not continue. It is hovering above the pad. It is replaced in the holder.

Then, without looking up, he starts his pack-up procedures.

I wait. Tense. I have not meant to sound so rude. It might not be his fault that the walls have next to no colour, and I guess it is not his fault that the plastic plant doesn't grow. But you can't take back what you've just said, if you meant it.

Abruptly he stands up.

'You're right, let's get out of here. I'd like you to help me choose a new suit and then I'll drive you home.'

I am bowled over. This man can change the direction of the wind with just a puff of words.

We walk down the street, talking about nice things. I don't mind if people think he is my dad. He looks important.

He asks if I am going to the kids' jazz bands concert in the Botanical Gardens on Saturday, who I'm going to go with, and how I am managing with the housekeeping chores now that Tessa is back.

I tell him about the omelette that Tessa thought was the best scrambled egg she had ever tasted and about Mrs Angle's tripe stew that looked like a pot of rotting rats' tails.

Tessa, I explain, has been home for a couple of days. She is getting better, but she doesn't look like she is. Her face and neck (I won't mention the rest of her body) are covered in weepy sores and scales left over from the disease. They will go, but she has got to rest, be quiet and not worry.

The doctor did not want to let her come home just yet. Said she should go to a rest home, maybe a health farm in the mountains away from the 'stresses of home life'. . . that's me.

Dr Jago seems to know what I mean. He nods like he agrees with that other doctor—that Tessa should really be kept away from her delinquent daughter.

'Don't go into her room unless you are delivering her meals,' her doctor had told me, like he was reprimanding a naughty toddler.

'Your mother,' he had instructed, 'must not be upset by you or she will get very, very sick indeed.'

Dr Jago seems to agree with that too. He is nodding. How would he know? He hasn't even seen Tessa since it happened.

I object, 'You haven't seen Tessa?'

'I'll pop in to see her when I drop you home. But first we must get this suit,' he says as we enter a very smart menswear shop.

'What can we do for you, Dr Jago?' the tailor says. He must be the owner because he has a tape measure around his neck, ready to make a quick sale.

'This little lady is going to help me choose a new suit. She is sick of seeing me in this colour,' Dr Jago replies.

'Nothing like a complete change,' the tailor says, walking over to the racks. 'You must have four like that one you have on.'

Dr Jago and the tailor disappear with several suits to try on. I take a seat. One of the shop assistants offers me a sweet in his fingers. I say no. His fingernails are a bit dirty. I am busy wondering how I can stop Dr Jago going in to see Tessa when he drops me home. I must think of something, she will die with humiliation.

She really looks ooowah yuk, and she would hate him to see her like that. She likes to look good for him, I know. She takes her good shoes in a bag to work on the days she has appointments with Dr Jago. Not a sane thing to do, but then he is her head shrinker.

The curtains spring open and there he is, in the same suit as he always wears, but in a different colour.

'How do you vote?' he asks me.

I have to nod, all eyes are on me. I now know why the courtiers said they liked the emperor's new clothes even though he was naked. There are times when it would be more that one's life is worth to disagree.

104

'I'll wear it,' Dr Jago says, 'nothing like a change to lift the spirit.'

'Change to lift the spirit,' somehow those words mean something to me. They are tailor-made to cause me trouble.

They zoom into my brain and they pound around and around, like a stuck record, bashing down the doors to hidden compartments, where there are files I have chosen to forget.

Memories are stirring, writhing, restless. I cannot keep them contained. And I don't want them any more, lying there in the back of my subconscious like vipers poised to attack.

In the car on the way home I just have to tell Dr Jago, I have to get these memories out of my head, let them escape, make them leave me, let me be *free* . . .

'We held a seance the night we ran away from Fat Head's party. It wasn't right; we shouldn't have done it—guess we wanted to see what happens, just once. Tessa must never know we did it, she would say it was just asking for trouble. I . . . I think Joel made contact with a bad spirit that night, and I don't think it ever left him.'

I am crying. Dr Jago stops the car.

'Tell me more,' he says, knowing now I will.

25

A seance can be a scary thing, even when you don't believe. It was Joel's idea. It was 8.30 p.m. when we escaped from Fat Head's party, because we couldn't bear to play Blind Man's Buff. Tessa was not due to pick me up till 11.30 p.m.

We had three hours to kill. Mr and Mrs Goldstein were not home. They had gone out for the night and were not expected back before midnight.

We knew we couldn't turn the lights on in the house because Mrs Connelly would see them from her kitchen window and would fetch us back to the party. So we just sat in the dark on the front verandah and giggled about silly things, like how big Kate's bum looks from behind, and how bad the records were (hardly the latest) and how Mrs Connelly's face would look if she could see us, hiding on the moonlit verandah.

Such a shriek. We were really relaxed. Benji went to get us a drink and opened tonic water instead of lemonade. He sweetened it up with a bit of something brown. I think it was brandy.

Then Joel suggested a seance. I had never been in one: none of us had. We all thought, 'Why not, why not?' Joel told us how he thought we should set ourselves up to attract the spirits.

Benji brought out the card table and I fetched the upright wooden kitchen chairs. Benji got one of Mrs Goldstein's card party tablecloths and smoothed it out.

Then, following Joel's instructions because he knew a lot about this kind of thing, Benji got a pad and pen, wrote all the letters of the alphabet and laid them in a big circle.

He kept the pad and pencil handy at the edge of the table to write down the gems of wisdom from communicating with astral beings.

The final thing we needed was something to spin in the centre of the table, and we chose a tonic bottle.

We were ready at last. It had taken some putting together in the dark. We positioned ourselves so that we sat like three points of a triangle. It works best that way—Joel's tip.

'Now we're ready. Let's concentrate,' said Joel, 'and don't move a muscle.'

Benji cleared his throat loudly. I thought I was going to burst with an impatient giggle, so I took the chance to clear my throat too and that relieved the pressure.

We wriggled our last wriggles. Then we were quiet.

Moonlight strobed onto the table where our fingertips rested oh so lightly on the cloth. Clouds floated fast through the skies, flicking pools of pale light around us.

'Clear your mind,' Joel told us. 'Think of nothing. Channel your energy into our seance. Let the power of the vibrations of the spiritual world travel through our hands to spell out their messages on our table.'

Something touched my leg. Aaaaahh! I screamed. I jumped. I upset the table. And then, after I'd done all those disturbing things, my brain began to work again and told me that the Goldsteins's cat had just brushed against me.

'Just my Lucky,' Joel laughed, 'Bet she knows what's going on. Black cats are super-sensitive. In fact, some people believe they have magic powers.'

'Black magic,' I whispered. Funny how the dark makes you whisper. 'Tessa is frightened of black cats. She crosses herself and expects bad luck if one crosses in front of her.'

Benji picked up the black cat and put it out the front door, then we spiritualists settled down again to the serious task of 'making contact' with celestial beings.

I told myself to control my wandering mind. I was winning for a while there, then Benji moved his leg against mine and the excitement was electrifying.

I kept a straight face, of course, and glared at the tonic bottle. He jiggled his leg. I moved my leg, 'cos I didn't know whether I was expected to do something next and I rationalised my action by noting that our touching under the table was cheating on Joel.

I had to concentrate. We had to give him our best. Joel wanted it to work, for something amazing to happen, for us to have an experience that was out of this world.

My heart beat fast. Joel began to breathe loudly and regularly. I got a bit scared. It was eerie and it seemed to be getting hotter even though the sun was probably looking at England at that time of our night.

'Your spin, Sally,' Joel said. And of course I spun, a weak twirl that slowly stirred the air and stopped on the letter N.

'Write that down for Sally,' said Joel.

Benji wrote it down on a page marked 'Messages for Sally'.

'Spin twelve more times,' Joel instructed.

Thirteen in all. That sounded spooky. But I did it, and these are the letters I got: NOSPLGTKESESZ.

'Your go, Benji,' Joel whispered.

I didn't want to look at Benji right then. Deep down I knew he felt like I did, that this sort of thing was ridiculous, absurd. Oh I hope Tessa does not find out: this would not get her blessing, 'cos it would not get God's blessing. At least, I don't think this sort of thing is encouraged by Father John. I wonder if I will have to confess it? I think I will pretend I did not know it was bad.

Benji spun, and spun and spun, and his message was about as meaningless as mine. No amount of rearranging makes anything of these letters: FOTLMYNONTELL.

Did I hear a sigh of relief at that time, or was it just in my mind?

I was frightened—frightened of being caught playing with God's world, trying to unlock the mysteries of life that we mortals are not meant to understand.

Joel spun, and a whizzer it was. Round and round and round it went till it finally flagged on: P. This was followed by S. And then followed by OEAKNOWRBUT.

A gust of wind rustled the leaves outside then tore through the wire fly screen to toss the letters of the alphabet into total disarray.

'That's it for the night,' said Benji. 'And we're none the wiser. What a lot of codswallop! This seance stuff only works if you fudge a bit, guide the bottle with a few little unnoticeable puffs of breath.'

Benji laughed so loud just thinking about cheating.

Meanwhile Joel was rearranging his letters in his head, this way, that way. And his face pulsated in the flashing moonlight, showing an expression as stern as a sphinx as he announced, 'I got a message. My thirteen letters spell: P.S. BREAK OUT NOW.'

26

January 22nd was Joel's sixteenth birthday. Oh boy, what a disaster. I'm even embarrassed remembering it in the presence of Miaow. Got to go well back in the diary, as I had only known them a few months then. Pre-code days.

Here it is:

Friday 21st.

Bought sunglasses for Joel. Kate and I took them to his house. He got them.

That is not the whole story. It is just a synopsis (I think that is what Mrs Barratt calls it)—just the bare bones of the story, all details reserved.

Now I must try to reconstruct the whole story and practise saying it out loud so that I can get it out of my system when I see Dr Jago this afternoon. He says regurgitating distasteful experiences will relieve my mental indigestion.

I take a deep breath and close my eyes. I'm thinking back.

But Tessa knocks on my bedroom door.

111

'Not too late with your homework, sweetheart. You're trying very hard now, I know. Kiss me before you put the light out,' she says.

Tessa will now have her ear against my door. I have seen her do that when I am not in the room and she thinks I am. I come out of the bathroom, say, and there she is, ear up against my door, eavesdropping into silence.

And when I say, 'Here I am, Mum,' (always loudly) she nearly freaks.

'Just wondering if you were using your typewriter,' she said once in a pathetic effort to cover her compromised position.

'Want to use it?' I asked, and she felt she had to nod. So I gave her the typewriter and she tapped away for hours (I listened with my ear up against *her* door).

Next morning, I found what she had typed. It looked like this:

qwerty io asdfgh kl;"zxcvbn ,./qwerty io asdfgh kl;"zxcvbnbn .

Lines and lines just like that, rows of letters just as they are on our keyboard. Poor Tessa, she can't type and she must have been cranky that some letters on our machine are stuck. I'm sure she won't ever ask about the typewriter again, thank goodness. Since that day I went bananas and tossed things around searching for my treasure box, it has even less letters operating.

Click. The bathroom door slides shut. Tessa has moved on.

I must think back now, I must order my thoughts so that I can tell Dr Jago about Joel's birthday.

Maybe Tessa has already told him about this event. I didn't attempt to disguise my meetings with Benji and Joel until after the Anzac Day disaster when I was made to 'realise that unsuitable friendships are a serious thing'.

Sure as eggs are eggs, it must have been Tessa who told Dr Jago about my Flame name. She first heard if from the Goldsteins, but then she would have had it confirmed when she read this diary.

I imagine she doesn't talk much about herself when she goes to see Dr Jago, wearing her best shoes, looking good.

She wouldn't want to say how hysterical and unreasonable she gets about little things—like, 'Why didn't you remind me to put the milk bottles out? Yes, I know it's my job, but you should have reminded me.'

I bet she keeps quiet about her twisted thinking. I imagine she sits cool, calm and collected in the manipulator's chair and talks about 'the little trouble-maker'—ME.

I must not think like that. Poisonous exaggeration is part of my sickness. That's what Dr Jago says.

'We're all trying to help you. Let us help you,' he says in soothing tones. 'Relax. Let it all out. Let me know what is troubling you. I can't help you if you keep me in the dark.'

Bad choice of words, I thought, After all, we're

talking about blindness. At least, I'm trying to.

I must practise talking about Joel's birthday, aloud.

'Dr Jago,' I will say, 'the night before Joel's birthday was a Friday night and I was staying over at Kate's house. Lots of kids stay with their best friend on a Friday night. Mothers don't seem to mind. They say: 'No homework? Okay, but don't stay up late.'

'Well, on our way home from school we went to the chemist to buy something for Joel. I hadn't seen him, or Benji, for a few weeks, but I had spoken to Benji on the phone. He used to ring up lots from public telephone boxes, until Tessa got thingy after the Anzac Day race meeting. He'd yak on till some impatient jerk would tip him out of the phone box.

'Anyway he told me it was Joel's sixteenth birthday coming up, and I felt so sorry for Joel when Benji told me that his mother would not be giving him a party.

'Strange really. That was something I could never understand because Joel was definitely her favourite.

'Joel was her jewel; he could do no wrong. That's the way I saw it. And Benji always got the blame for everything.

'I think it was 'cos she couldn't be cross with a blind boy, like he was extra fragile and had to be protected from the morale bruising of her ear-bashing.

'Benji told me that she used to say: "Think of your brother first; we must all put him before ourselves. He has suffered enough."

'That is why it surprised me that he wasn't going

114

to have a party—it would have been a chance for his friends to make him feel special without feeling they were patronising him.

'So, to cut a long story short, Kate helped me choose a present.

'We went to the chemist and couldn't think of anything. The shop girl suggested talcum powder for men, some special deodorant, some aftershave stuff . . . all so personal and impossible.

'Then we saw the stand with sunglasses and I began to think, just slowly at first, that they would be a good idea.

'I've seen many blind people wearing sunglasses all day and all night, like Stevie Wonder, and it's cool.

'Kate agreed that Joel would be good-looking with dark glasses.

'We tried many pairs on. We got a better idea on Kate's face because she could look more like him. My orange halo made it difficult to imagine his face.

'Many people came in while we were deciding and they offered "helpful" opinions. It didn't matter, because they thought the glasses were for Kate herself.

'We had the chosen pair gift-wrapped and decided to pop the little package into Joel's letterbox after dark so we wouldn't be seen by his parents. Neither of us had ever met them, didn't even know what they looked like.

'So at last light we walked to Benji and Joel's house, not far from Kate's place. We were really happy, and giggly. And just a little nervous, I think. Any little thing would start us giggling, but we sobered up when we came to the Goldsteins's house.

'The curtains were wide open and we could see the dinner table laid so nicely. You could see at a glance it was not a casual dinner.

'A woman came in and faced the table. She put her hands over her eyes for a few moments, saying a prayer I think, and then she lit the two candles on the table. She straightened some of the cutlery and left the room.

'Kate and I looked at each other. "Mrs Goldstein?" I suggested. Kate nodded. We were both guessing.

'Without saying anything to each other, we crouched low, peering through the hedge, magnetised by this picture-window view into the Goldsteins's lives.

'Joel came to the verandah screen door. My heart began to bang and I think I heard Kate's too. He lent out and called, "Lucky, Lucky, Lucky . . . Lucky, Lucky, Lucky."

'We held our breath. There was a rustle behind us, the cat shot between us, through the hedge, across the lawn and into Joel's arms. Then he went inside.

' "We had better go," Kate whispered, pulling me out into the open again. She took the parcel and slipped it into the mail box. Just as she did this, a family with two girls our age faced us. They were going to the Goldsteins.

' "Something I can take in?" said the mother, and

took the package out of the box. "I'll give it to him," she said, reading that it was for Joel. And in they went.

'Kate and I were frozen with humiliation. We wanted to run and yet we had to stay. Slowly we crept back to our possie in behind the hedge and we watched.

'After an age the families filed into the dining room and shuffled around for a while till they found their place at the table.

'Then I saw that woman put our package on Joel's plate. Oh heaven, help us? Kate and I were rigid. The mozzies were biting, but they didn't hurt that night.

'The one we thought was Mrs Goldstein came in and gave all the men and boys little round hats like coloured pikelets, and they put them on their heads. They must have been one short, so the man visitor put his paper napkin on his head.

' "*Some party!*" I whispered to Kate, but she knew all about it. This was the Shabbat dinner, she explained, the Friday night meal that marks the beginning of the Jewish Sabbath, which falls every Saturday. For Roman Catholics, the day of rest is Sunday, and Tessa usually adheres to that.

'Mr Goldstein read from a small book. Then he lifted a white cloth off a plaited loaf of bread, broke the bread into small pieces and handed a piece to everyone.

'He sipped from a silver goblet and passed that round too, before they all sat down and Mrs Goldstein went out of the room.

'In the long, silent moments that Kate and I were experiencing, Joel "looked straight" ahead while the

117

others were moving their heads around, chatting.

'Then Joel put his hands on his plate. Our hearts stopped and the conversations seemed to cease as everyone watched Joel unwrap our package.

'He put the sunglasses on. Everyone peered at him. Mrs Goldstein wheeled back in with a trolley of serving dishes. She saw Joel and abandoned the trolley; one hand clasped her mouth and the other stole the wrapping paper off Joel's lap.

'The others seemed pleased with the effect. They started smiling and talking to Joel, but Mrs Goldstein fumbled for her reading glasses, then puzzled over the unsigned inscription:

"For good-looking Joel, from mystery admirers."

'We fled.'

27

'We didn't see much of each other in the months that followed, probably because our parents weren't friends,' I tell Dr Jago.

He could be listening to me, but he doesn't look like it. He is staring out the window with his mind near Mars. Oh well, I get into less trouble if I talk than if I don't talk—and what's it to me if he's bored?

'Tessa,' I continue, 'tried hard to stop me thinking about the Goldsteins because she said it would all come to a sticky end. I bet she remembers saying that, and someday she won't be able to resist saying "I warned you, I warned you."

'Anyway, she made it her business to try and tee me up with nerds you wouldn't be seen dead with. They were always sons of her church-going friends and medical curiosities to the world of orthodonists, orthopaedists and dermatologists. Yes, they had lots of sticking-out teeth, sticking-out bones and sticking-out zits. You name it, they were bodies 'OUT OF ORDER'.

Dr Jago smiles just a little. I think he is listening.

'So, to be with Benji at all, I used Kate as a cover-up. That suited Kate because she got included. Then, of course, we had Joel tagging along too, just to keep Mrs Goldstein happy.

After I had said that, I knew how mean it sounded.

Dr Jago asks, 'Did Benji feel resentful of his brother's presence?'

'Sure he did, sometimes,' I say. 'Mrs Goldstein sort of didn't want Benji to have any fun that Joel might miss out on. She wouldn't hear of Joel being left to do something on his own.

'Benji said to me once, "Wouldn't it be beaut if just us two could be together, but that won't be possible."

'He explained that his mother insisted it was his responsibility to see that Joel did not miss out. "He has suffered enough," she reminded Benji often. And she was right, but Benji was not allowed to have a mind of his own. "Look after your brother," she would say to Benji every morning as they left for the bus, "and bring him home safely." '

Dr Jago notes, 'That was a big responsibility. Was Joel happy with this enforced dependency?'

'I think he must have hated being tied to his brother at times, just like Benji felt trapped. Benji's job in life seemed to be his blind brother's minder.

'Don't get me wrong. We all loved Joel. The day we all went to Funfair Park we had a top time together.'

I smile thinking of it. Dr Jago is watching me.

'Did you ride on The Big Diver?' he probes.

'Huh? Yeah. Twice,' I tell him. 'One time sitting next to Benji and one time sitting next to Joel.

'I don't know whether it is best to look or not look when The Big Diver plunges and plummets. I tried it both ways and I screamed both times.

'Kate and Benji screamed all the time too, but Joel did not make a sound. He had the self-discipline of a kamikaze pilot.'

Dr Jago's eyebrows move, upwards. I think he liked the thought of The Big Diver as a suicidal thrill.

Now his moustache is wriggling, a warning that words are about the come out.

'Whose decision was it to go on The Big Diver for a second ride?' he asks.

What a silly question. I answer sternly. 'We all did. We liked being frightened.' That put Dr Jago back in his box.

Sometimes I think Dr Jago lives life through other people. He doesn't have to leave this lifeless room to experience the world—he just finds out about it through his patients.

'What else did you enjoy there?' he persists.

'Well now,' I think a bit, 'the hamburger, the fairy floss, the dodgem cars, and the, oh yes, the talent quest. Benji went in it. There was a band on a small stage and they were hip. We watched for a bit. Then they said, "Talent time, who've we got? Come on, come on, do anything and we'll give you two tickets to see the Mighty Martians—just the best band."

121

' "Wow!" we said, just to ourselves. Then Kate suggested that Benji do a number 'cos he is really good—guitar, singing, you name it. He didn't want to be in it, but Kate's got the biggest mouth and she shouted, "Benji Goldstein." '

'And?' Dr Jago prods.

'He was great, just great. He sang and played guitar. He was sort of looking at me, and all the girls around were clapping along. He won the tickets. He gave them to me.

'But we didn't see The Mighty Martians concert. By the time they arrived in Sydney, the flame had gone out.'

'What's that?' queries Dr Jago. 'What flame?'

He's got me cornered, squealing home truths like a traitor during torture. Mind-benders have a knack that is not by chance.

From the bottom of my heart, I squeeze the strength to tell him. I remind myself that I've got to tell Dr Jago the hardest things or I'll never get better. That's what he says. That's what Tessa says.

Tell him, tell him everything . . .

'You know those fun fair stalls where you shoot the moving ducks and everyone wins a prize? Well, Joel got a high score by accident, just by pressing the trigger—bang, bang, bang—and Benji tried hard and got a low score.

'Joel chose a big stuffed tiger toy from the top shelf of prizes and Benji took, without hesitation, the little heart-shaped kerosene lamp with "You light up my

122

life" on it. He asked for a match and lit the wick.

'It burned with the silliest little flame, but it looked pretty. Kate said to Benji, "Why didn't you get the plastic flowers, at least they could be useful." She is so *tactless*.

'Later, when she wasn't looking, Benji gave the lamp to me. "That flame is just like your ponytail," he said. "And," he whispered, "I mean what it says on it. You are my flame, and that's what I'm going to call you." '

28

On the way home, Benji explained my new name to Joel. He described my orange ponytail flaring out like the flame that follows spacecraft as they leave this earth.

'I'll call her Flame too,' Joel suggested, and from that day on they both called me Flame. I stopped hating my hair. I almost liked it.

They said that my hair made me unique. I looked that word up in the dictionary just to know exactly what I meant to them.

Seems I was: the only one of my kind, having no like or equal, standing alone in comparison with others, unequalled, remarkable, rare and unusual.

That is some consolation for having the sort of hair people have to touch when they sit behind you in the cinema! Oohwaahh, I hate that!

The only times I didn't mind that light, testing touch were the times when Joel made 'body contact', as he called it. His inquiring touch was quite delicate, his feel so feathery that, even when he had searched my body from head to toe, I did not feel he had intruded on my privacy.

Blind people really need to explore outside their own world. How can we understand how trapped they must feel in their black world? Benji explained this to me, and I've tried to understand.

We all three made 'body contact' the day we walked to the lighthouse. It was a bad day to go, blustery and cold, but when you decide to go you have to go, especially when you haven't got other days to put it off to.

The climb to the lighthouse is difficult, and we had to have Joel in between us, telling him where to put each foot. That was no problem. We were used to doing things as a team.

Joel wore his sunglasses. He never did ask me if I gave them to him. His way of thanking me was to wear them when we went out together.

Finally, we got to the top and it was horrible. The sea mist was rising from the smashed waves below and floating like a fog to shroud the view.

We hurried into a sheltered cave on the far cliff, disturbing a huddle of seagulls. They left, somewhat indignant, wailing discordant sounds as they winged out into the turbulent thermals.

We were puffed. We laughed and snorted and snivelled a bit, our noses dribbling, our hair so messed by the wicked wind. It was a stupid place to be on such an awful day.

I brought out some sandwiches. Joel produced a little

radio that could do no more than crackle like dry grass in a bushfire. And Benji got out his harmonica, but the little tune he blew was lost to the wind.

Then I saw the furry bundle, tucked up in a corner of the cave. At first I thought it was dead because it lay so still.

'Look at that, Benji,' I said, and he turned to where I pointed.

'Shoo!' he shouted, but it did not move. He reached out for a stick that lay nearby and used it to turn the tiny creature over.

Then we could see it was a bat, the flying fruit fox kind, with a furry little body and smooth jointed wings, in size no bigger than a large rat.

It made just the slightest movements with the little life it had left in it. It was too sick to fly.

'Oooooo-yuk,' I bawled. 'It's disgusting. I hate bats. They carry germs galore and they get tangled in people's hair. Chuck it.'

'It's nearly dead,' Benji said, picking it up very carefully.

I looked more closely, and it didn't look so dangerous. Benji put it on his lap and stretched out its wings—one was broken and the poor creature had probably lain there for days, starving to death.

On closer inspection, the bat's face was cute. I hadn't realised that bats are furry and soft. I patted it as Benji prepared to wrap it in his raincoat.

At that moment, Joel put his hand out.

'Show me,' he said impatiently, 'I want to see it.'

Benji looked up, surprised by his tone. We handed the bat to Joel. He took it in both hands, and it wriggled just enough to prove it was alive.

Joel held it in one cupped hand and set about discovering its shape with the other.

If I close my eyes, I can still see Joel 'looking' at that bat. He felt every bone in its long flexible wings, he stirred his fingertips through the thick fur, he separated each of the ten strong toes, and he found its sightless eyes.

At the time I said to him, 'Bet you know more about that bat now than we do. Hey, Benji?'

Benji confirmed, 'There is no telling what he finds out.'

I suggested, 'Let's try closing our eyes and being blind and seeing how much we can see.'

'Good one, Flame, find out about me first,' Benji enthused. 'I'll keep my eyes shut too.'

I shuffled over to where Benji was. I shut my eyes and I moved my hands over his head and down his neck, just like Joel did to me that first time in the bus stop shelter. I had trouble keeping my eyes shut; they kept peeping.

I touched his face, went down and up his arms and then down to his waist. When I got there, I tickled him.

It was a fun game. We laughed. I admitted I peeped at times, and Benji started looking for something we could use as a blindfold.

I suggested we have two blindfolds so no one could

cheat at any time. Benji took off his long socks and wrapped one around my head.

It *stank*. And I said so.

Errruugghh!

Joel was listening to us, sensing exactly what was going on.

'My turn?' he asked, tucking the limp, dying bat inside his coat.

'As long as you don't cheat,' I said. 'Who do you want to start on first?'

'I'll warm up with Flame,' he joked.

I moved beside Joel.

He put his hands on my lap. They moved down my thighs, slow and deliberate, round my calves and on down to my ankles. He pulled off my short gumboots and felt every toe like each one was 'unique' (my new word).

While this was happening I felt very self-conscious —my mind kept visualising what two people doing what we were doing in broad daylight would look like if seen by a working human eye.

Joel would not have had that distracting image, because he had no experience of what two people looked like in reality.

'My turn,' interrupted Benji. He was boisterously enthusiastic. 'Move over here, Flame. I'll start with your feet—that way I can be sure things will get better.'

He, too, was blindfolded with a smelly sock.

His style of feeling was quite different to Joel's— his hands bounced and slithered suggestively, his

128

fingers marched with a jaunty touch forever upwards, over my knees, onto my hips, round my waist . . . till he reached my chest, where the palms of his hands landed flat and firm on my boobs.

I froze. Rigid. I kept my eyes so tightly shut I think my eyeballs moved back into the brain area. My brain, I have to admit, was completely out of action at the time—it was disconnected and no messages were getting in or out.

Benji pressed a bit, then he squeezed subtly, just like Tessa tests peaches when Mario, the Friendly Fruitologist, is not looking.

'Checking they are ready to eat,' is her excuse every time.

My heart began to race. He would have felt that; his fingers were right on the pulse.

I slapped his hands away. After all, we were not supposed to be feeling what is inside the other person. We were only meant to explore the outside shape.

Joel was all around us at that moment. I could feel him 'looking' at us, silently, sensitively.

Benji's lips touched mine, just a wispy tickle, but it made my genitals tingle and my heart stop completely.

Joel's voice jolted us, restarting my heart with a kick.

He said, 'While you have been playing the game, the bat has died.'

Benji and I took off our blindfolds. "I'll chuck it," Benji said, trying to take it from Joel.

'No, we'll do it together,' he said, holding tight to the bat. 'Lead me to the edge of the cliff.'

So we stood either side of Joel, our eyes screwed up as we faced the biting wind.

'Little blind one, follow the light of our God,' Joel said, and he tossed the bat.

29

Lifesaver's new hard hat is now covered with bird shit. I suggest that he takes it off next time it rains and leave it on top of the rock ledge.

'This hat protects my head,' he points out wisely, 'and if I took it off, I would risk having a head that looks like the hat.' Lifesaver cackles like a crazy man.

One-leg One and One-leg Two give out a victorious squawk . . . and an extra-big squirt. I shudder. Ooo-yuk!

I have Tessa's shopping with me. I give Lifesaver an apple and a banana from Mario's fruit bag. I hope Tessa doesn't know how many pieces of each kind of fruit make a kilo.

Oh dear . . . now Lifesaver throws half of what I give him to his birds. Tessa will never know that.

'How are your actors shaping up?' I ask. 'You know, the ones that rehearse in your head?'

'Oh, fine, dear. We are nearly ready to raise the curtain, and then you'll learn a thing or two.'

'What's the lesson?' I ask.

'Long-range forecasting. Yes, you'll learn about the future, about the forces of inevitable fate.'

'But most people can't understand their past; why worry them with the future?' I puzzle.

'Your past will be explained by knowing your future. Mystery events will have meaning. They will be seen as part of an individual pattern, predetermined for each soul at birth.'

'Oh, Lifesaver, you are confusing me more,' I protest. 'I'm already bonkers. Did you know I go to . . . a head-shrinker?'

'Good on you,' he replies. 'I used to go to one, way back, and he fixed me up just fine. You might be lucky too.'

30

Dr Jago was really quite interested to know I had gone to Benji's Bar Mitzvah, the Jewish ceremony when a boy becomes a member of the adult Jewish community.

'Were you invited?' he asks, puzzled.

'Nope,' I admit.

He shakes his head slightly and, still perplexed, he asks, 'How did you know what to do?'

'Joel told me, of course. He told me everything about it. I asked him after I saw this man they call the rabbi come out of the Goldsteins's house one day when Kate and I were walking down to the shops.

'Joel explained that the rabbi went to their house once a week for a long time teaching Benji the laws of their religion, the meaning of all their calendar events, the Hebrew language and all the things he has to know before he can become a fully responsible adult at the Bar Mitzvah ceremony.

'Joel told me that it was a day Jewish boys never forget. Benji was a little older than most Bar Mitzvah

133

boys, but the family had been waiting for some close relatives from Europe to be with them on this important day.

'He explained that the day starts for the Bar Mitzvah boy with participation in the service at the synagogue. Later that day, or in the evening, the parents of the boy throw a big party for relatives and close friends.

'Naturally I wanted to go. D'you blame me?' I say, with a note of defiance in my voice.

'Not at all,' Dr Jago agrees. 'It is a great occasion to see, especially when you know how much it means to the Bar Mitzvah boy. Tell me, did Benji know you were there?'

'Nope. You see, I didn't want him to be embarrassed that he hadn't asked me officially. I was sort of hurt when I first heard that they were going to have a big party. But when I went to the ceremony, I realised I didn't understand what it was all about.

'I didn't, and I still don't, understand about being Jewish. I guess Benji didn't understand about being Catholic.'

Dr Jago rubs his moustache. Unless he asks me a question, I can't think of any more to tell him, about anything.

'What did you wear to the synagogue?' he asks.

'I dressed up in my Sunday dress. Honestly,' I say, frustrated, 'do you want to know all the nitty-gritty details? Like how did I wear my hair? And where did I sit? etc. etc.? Do you?'

'Yes,' he says emphatically. 'I am very interested.'

I sigh the squeaky sigh of a wrung-out sponge as the last drops of water are forced into the sink.

I tell him, 'I went to the synagogue wearing a scarf tied tightly around my head so that not one strand of orange hair could give away my identity. I arrived at 9.15 a.m., just fifteen minutes after the service commenced, so that I couldn't possibly run into the Goldsteins.

'I took the flight of stairs to the left of the front door, which led to the entrance of the first-floor gallery where women and girls must take their place.

'I got to that door without having to look at anyone. Joel's instructions were perfect.

'Carefully, I opened the door to the gallery, lowered my head and crept to the closest pew.'

Dr Jago has his tape machine going. He is going to be disappointed. This is not an action-packed story.

'Mmmh, mmmhh,' he encourages me.

'I knew where to look for Benji 'cos Joel had described what goes on. The men and boys were all on the ground floor, with the rabbi and his helpers in the centre and two Bar Mitzvah boys close by.

'All the men and boys were wearing those pikelet caps, kippot they are called. Someone in very fancy robes was chanting and many of the men in the pews chatted quietly to each other. That never happens in the Catholic Church—we're expected to be quiet, unless we're participating in prayer or song.

'Joel was there on the sidelines sitting next to the man who wore the paper napkin on his head that night

135

before Joel's birthday. Mr Goldstein, the one who broke the bread that night, was sitting with Benji.

'From where they were sitting, Benji could not see me. I began to relax and, although it was all in Hebrew at that stage and I couldn't understand a word, it was colourful to look at and intriguingly different from our church service.

'I was wondering why Benji kept this part of his life such a secret. He never mentioned being Jewish or what he did on Saturdays.

'The Bar Mitzvah boys then stood up and walked to where the rabbi was standing. He was saying, in English now, "The customs and traditional Judaic laws, as told to us in the teachings of our holy Torah, must be observed to achieve our earthly destiny and eternal salvation as designed for us by God, sole creator of this universe."

'The way the rabbi spoke was really impressive. I was just thinking how sad it was that Benji had not shared with me thoughts about his religion, because I could already see ways it was similar to mine, when I noticed Mrs Goldstein staring at me.

'Her glare made me understand instantly why Benji had hidden this part of his life from me.

'Why she noticed, and focused on me that day in the synagogue I will never know. Maybe a sixth sense, or something like that, told her there was *danger* in the room.

'Silly really, because we were just knock-about friends. It was before we were close. I had not even met Mrs Goldstein, but she reacted like a mother elephant who has caught a whiff of a distant lion— she was alert, tense, defensive.

'Yes, that's it, Mrs Goldstein looked at me as if I was threatening her babies, like I had to be frightened away.

'And the women around her seemed to sense her predicament. They cast their protective glares, too. Or, at least, I thought they did.

'Their looks attacked my nerves. I tugged at the scarf. It slipped off. My orange mane flared out. I was exposed, out in the open, looking like that predatory lion, but feeling like a frightened gazelle.

'I couldn't stay there any longer. I fled for cover. I ran home to *my* mother.'

31

It wouldn't have been kind to tell Dr Jago that I met Tessa sooner than I expected. As I rushed from the synagogue I ran slap-bang into Tessa, who was walking with a man.

You see, Tessa is so fragile these days, since the shingles, and it would be awful if Dr Jago used my information and asked Tessa at her next session, 'Who was this man Sally saw you with?'

Miaow knows about him. Don't you, Miaow? I had to tell someone that day. Miaow want her tummy rubbed? Poor Miaow, you must get sick of listening to my tangled mind.

I didn't even mention that brief encounter in my diary, because I think the man is her secret, not mine. I have seen her with him one other time—that was a day I was piking school. Yes, he was the one I had seen her with outside the synagogue. I think he is too old for her, and he should be told that sideburns went out centuries ago.

Mind you, meeting me as I ran out from the

synagogue must have aged Tessa. She wanted to say, 'Explain yourself,' but she couldn't really in her awkward situation.

My scarf was the giveaway, and she snatched the hand-out I was holding which detailed the Bar Mitzvah service.

'Go home,' she said, her voice trembling, her expression stunned.

'I was,' I insisted, aggressively, as I backed off. I wasn't ready to meet a man who might take Dad's place. It was such a shock; painful for both of us.

Tessa has never mentioned that meeting again, and she hasn't brought that fellow into my life.

Perhaps he isn't a good Catholic?

32

Joel's week of work experience would make being unemployed seem like an attractive career.

His school had contacted various industries and offices in our area, asking if they would take a pupil for a five-day working week and introduce them to their line of business.

Joel got sent to a light-fitting manufacturer not far from my school, and the task he was given was to fit light bulbs into sockets.

The job, and I just cringe remembering it, meant nothing to Joel, and it was both ironic and cruel to give it to a blind boy.

The manager of the factory didn't mean to insult him, I'm sure. Joel said that everyone working there was welcoming and kind—so protective of him, in fact, that his workmates insisted on taking it in turns to accompany him to the bathroom, and they would to stand by him while he had a pee.

One day, just after I got home from school, Joel rang from the factory.

'Come and get me, Flame, will you? I've told them I'm sick and that my sister will take me home. That's you. Okay?'

I ran all four blocks to the factory and found Joel sitting beside the receptionist slumped over, holding his stomach.

'Joel, I'm here, I'm here,' I said, rushing to touch him. I put my hand on his shoulder and, like magic, he uncurled and rose.

As we started towards the door, the manager came out of his office.

'Our Joel is a proud man,' he said, 'He would not let me drive him home. Are you two sure you are all right now? Feeling a bit better now, lad? Nice to be with your loved ones when you're not one hundred per cent.'

We left. That man and my best friend Kate have a similar way with words. God should strike them both dumb.

Joel shuffled along the first block, but when we turned the corner he whooped with joy.

'Bloody marvellous, I'm *free*,' he shouted, vibrating with delight.

What he said next, I will never forget: 'You have helped me free my body from that factory. Now will you help me free my soul from this body?'

I was shocked. His words were soaking in, but oh so slowly.

He caught me by the shoulders and held me, facing him. His fingertips, toughened with tension, dug into

141

my flesh. He was like a man possessed, obsessed, carried away with the desperate need to find a meaning to life, to be convinced that there is something more to life than (dare I say it?) meets the eye.

From my point of view, and this is the line I took in the school debate about life after death, this afterlife question has been asked and unanswered since God created man, and eons of argument will not reveal a truth.

Not here on the pavement, in factory land, at 3.30 p.m., to two school kids!

'Let's have a milkshake down at the milk bar,' I suggested. 'Waffles would be nice, with caramel sauce. Want some? Come on, Joel, snap out of it. I hate the way you get uptight about all this. You make life a misery for yourself.'

I didn't mean that. But I had just said it. Funny how your mouth can talk sometimes without checking with the brain first.

His grip eased and his arms fell to his sides. I took his hand and we started off. I chatted, 'Just as well I've got my pocket money with me. I take it with me now all the time in case we get robbed while I am at school and Tessa is at work.

'If they ever come though, I hope they take the typewriter that is under my bed. I wouldn't want to type if it ends me up in a job like that girl at that desk in the factory. She looked so bored and cooped up. Ohhh!'

Joel used my innocent words to mean things he wanted them to say.

'You don't need to be cooped up, imprisoned in earthbound situations. If we humans train our minds through the various disciplines of yoga and meditation, we can find our souls and release them to travel anywhere in extraterrestrial spheres.'

'And meet people like E.T.?' I joke.

'Yes, yes,' he said, apparently pleased I was going along with him. 'Who knows what other celestial creatures we may meet? The spirit world exists, Flame—it exists for me, you can read it in the stars. It can exist for you, even if you don't believe now.

'Don't knock it, Flame. Help me find it!'

He was so insistent, so pathetic. Just looking at him, it was obvious that he had been denied so much in life. It wasn't my place to deny him hope that there was something better in store.

'Sure, I'll listen,' I agree.

Over the milkshakes and waffles Joel cheered up and spoke about astral spirit travel and like ideas with the conviction of a latter-day Joan of Arc.

'You see, there are three parts to us—the body, the soul and the intellect,' he explained. 'The body is something you can cut up, do an autopsy on, find out exactly how it works.

'But,' he went on loudly, 'you can't cut up a thought. An idea is intangible, but you cannot deny that it is *real*!'

This sort of talk scared the living daylights out of

me. I wished Benji was with us—he knew how to handle Joel when he got wound up like this.

The people at the table next door were listening. I didn't blame them. It is not every day that one can overhear this kind of conversation in a milk bar. Or anywhere for that matter.

I didn't want them to hear me say 'Yes, yes', in case they thought I was agreeing with him, so I found myself nodding encouragement.

'Are you listening?' Joel asked so loudly, adjusting his dark glasses.

'Let's talk about this somewhere else,' I whispered. 'I'm er, I'm er . . . feeling too hot in here.'

We walked out and down the street. He asked me, 'Just one more favour? Take me to the bookshop in Phillip Street. You can help me find some good reading.'

What a relief. I thought I had distracted him from his obsession but, when we got there, the bookshop had (probably still has) a section under the heading 'New Age Literature'. It has to be seen to be believed.

There on the shelves was a Himalayan mountain of occult books covering every weirdo branch of spiritualism and related crazy practices, including subjects such as: faith healing, spoon bending, unidentified flying objects, astral travel, tarot card reading, self-exploration through meditation, yoga, the healing powers of crystals, the meaning of past lives, psychokinesis, spirit manifestations, ghosts, psychic surgery, transmigration of souls, and

144

parapsychology . . . to name just a few!

'Read me some titles,' said Joel. 'I'll buy you a book and then you'll understand more.'

Just to keep him happy, I chose *The World of Psychic Phenomena*. As Joel paid for it, I tried to imagine how I would keep it hidden from Tessa. She would go berserkers if she thought I was getting into this stuff.

As we left the shop he said, 'Got something mind-bending lined up for next week, want to come along?'

'Mmmmhhh,' I hesitate.

He went on, 'Going to a channelling session with a psychic medium. It will be scary, but we might meet spirits.'

'Wow!' I said. Help! I thought.

33

Of course, Joel could not get to the spirit medium's house unless I took him.

Benji, by this time, was totally fed up with Joel's 'search for a third eye—his inner everlasting soul', and would do nothing to encourage Joel's interest in occult practices.

'It is one thing,' Benji said, 'to go to these seance shows with an open mind, and quite another to go like Joel, determined to believe.'

Benji felt that Joel was now mentally gullible to auto-suggestion by any persons claiming extrasensory powers and that he would fall for any tricks these 'fake artists fiddle'.

I wasn't too sure how strong I was either, especially when the moment of no return came as we knocked on the medium's front door.

Goodness knows where Joel got her address or the gen about her.

He knew she was famous for her trumpet sittings, when the spirits supposedly 'channelled' their messages

146

through her and their voices came out of trumpets.

The light above her front door was green, and it made Joel look horrible. We could hear muffled steps inside and we waited and waited, but they did not come to the door until we knocked again, very loudly.

'Oh, my pets,' she said with surprise when our message finally got through to her. 'Next time just come right in. I'm almost deaf to sounds that have to travel through the tympanic membrane, but, as you will soon see, I can pick up signals from outer space.

'You may know who I am. I am Madame Star, clairvoyant and medium of repute, but I must not know who you are or why you have come here. The messages we may receive for you tonight must have no meaning to me.'

She ushered us in. 'Sit here among your fellow spiritualists, tell not a word about yourselves, sit quietly, relax and fine-tune your sensitivity till we are sure all our participants are here.'

The room was dimly lit with just one lamp in the corner, shrouded by an embroidered shawl similar to those worn by gypsies.

Madame Star was grossly overweight, her huge body draped in a kaftan. Each step she took created vibrations that made the fleshy rolls of her body gyrate.

Joel and I sat down together on a tiny stool. I wanted to tell Joel what the room was like, how spooky the whole place looked, how disgustingly obese Madame Star was, how the toenails of her bare feet were long and curly . . .

147

We ought to have scrammed right then and there. But he couldn't see the details and we didn't scram.

For some time, Madame Star kept disappearing and reappearing through a black curtain into the next room. The six others waiting with us were a mixed bunch. I wanted to know what they really looked like, so I could perhaps guess why they were there. But, strangely, all faces were fuzzed by the intimidating stillness of that room.

Finally, Madame Star came in with a small homemade-looking trumpet and sat it upturned on the floor in the middle of the room. Then she left.

The lady on my right opened her handbag and jingled her money bag. Everyone got the message, including Joel, who gave me what looked like more than I get in a whole year for pocket money. He asked me to 'make this our donation'.

'You must be joking,' I hissed. 'How much is here?'

'The amount she asked me to bring. Don't worry yourself; you are my guest,' Joel said, giving my leg a pat.

I did like the others, dropped it in the trumpet. But, unlike the others, I already felt conned. What would we get for all that money?

Madame Star called us into the other room after we had all paid up . . . and just after the one who had jingled the money had given a high-pitched sneeze.

Was she an accomplice of Madame Star?

Two large candles burned on either side of the bulk in black that was Madame Star. They highlighted the chairs arranged in a circle and we all took a place.

When my eyes got used to the dark I saw three trumpet shapes at Madame Star's feet, each topped with its own distinctively patterned band of iridescent tape.

Her helper, the money-jingler, moved silently on her bare feet over to the candles and she snuffed them out.

The minutes that followed were especially long—we were left alone with our personal panic.

Madame Star's breathing got louder and deeper as she worked herself into a hypnotic trance. Then her voice boomed with terrifying immediacy.

'Take hands around the circle, share the energy of your combined souls to create an atmosphere congenial to the supernatural world, so that we here may have the benefit of the the wise and benevolent thoughts of our astral guides.'

I squeezed Joel's hand. He squeezed mine back. I don't know what that gesture meant to him, but it kept me sane.

'Let us not walk the path of life in darkness,' she went on, her voice now taking on a chanting tone, 'but show us your light, dear God, through the tutelage of spectral beings who are part of the great universal intelligence.'

Oh *help*! The room was getting hot. There were no windows open, in fact no sign of a window. That meant I was probably breathing in the very air that Madame Star was puffing out. *Ooohh yuk*!

I started to take less breaths and hold them as long as I could. That wasn't a clever idea, because holding your breath lots makes you kind of dizzy.

I was beginning to feel fuzzy in the head just before the trumpets started to rise . . . and sway . . . this way and that, just above head height. Their visible bands now were the only thing we could see in the room.

A squeaky voice started whining through the octaves and seemed to be coming out of one of the trumpets, but I knew it had to be Madame Star doing her ventriloquist act.

The clipped Irish accent talked gibberish for a while, then Madame Star interrupted.

'There is a sceptic in the room, one who is fighting the spirit world, fending off contact from outer space, offending our faithful communicators. Let such a person capitulate . . . or leave this room.'

That had to be *me* she was referring to. I was the disbeliever. I just *couldn't* believe. But I had to try. I didn't have the courage to leave the room, showing that I thought they were self-deluding fools. They would have hated me. And my leaving would have caused Joel sharp pain.

I said to myself, 'Believe, believe, believe, believe.' That was the best I could do. I kept saying that over and over, like a meditation chant, so my rebellious thoughts couldn't get to the front of my brain and be detected.

It worked. The Irish voice returned, confident and confidential.

'I have messages from dear ones for people who have shown great faith and patience in their endeavours to make contact. Those loved ones now in the spirit world are eternally grateful for your continuing love. They want to say that the efforts you undertake to refine your souls while you are earthbound will be rewarded in the hereafter. You will reach higher planes of consciousness not achieved by less-developed souls.'

All three trumpets moved around a little then. Something brushed my shoulder. Someone brushed my shoulder?

'Believe, believe, believe, believe,' I had to say to myself to override that disbelieving 'thought' that just knocked against my shoulder. I would hate her to single me out again.

The trumpet with the zigzag band then took the centre of the circle announcing in a strange Asian lilt, 'I am Tampopito, a shogun of ancient Japan, a ruler with a past both glorious and glorified. I am here, knowing all, to answer your questions. Seek guidance and enlightenment from the knowledge shared in the world of harmonic existence.'

The voice trilled and the trumpet vibrated.

Someone asked, 'How old are you?'

'In our reality, we have no time,' said Tampopito.

'Why are you making your presence known to man?' asked the woman sitting across from me.

'Because you are ready now . . .'

'Is the world about to end?' asked a nervous participant.

'No, in a word, no. This is not the ending. This is the begi. . . gi. . . i . . . aachoooo' (a shuddering, high-pitched sneeze violently shook the trumpet).

'Beginning,' said Madame Star's voice, finishing off the sentence for the feverish Tampopito.

After that, I swear I heard little wiping-nose sounds coming from somewhere behind me. And it was a sneeze in the same pitch as the money-jingler's earlier sneeze.

'Bless you, Tampopito,' I said, quite spontaneously. Tessa always says that after someone sneezes.

And then I couldn't resist asking the once mighty warlord, 'Do ghosts get colds?'

34

'Joel became bitter when I told him that Madame Star was a fraud, but I had to tell him for his own good, didn't I?'

Dr Jago seems reluctant to reply.

Things have definitely changed around here from the early therapy sessions when Dr Jago did most of the prodding and probing, and I remained stubbornly incommunicative.

Now he sits, smugly triumphant, just watching and listening as I untangle the knot of painful memories I tied up so tight the first day I read the headline:

YOUNG BROTHERS
JUMP TO DEATHS:
LOVED SAME GIRL

Ohhh, ohhh. I never thought I would *ever* be able even to think those words aloud in my head. I must be getting better. I must go on. Go on, go on, go on . . .

'Wasn't it a good idea to tell him?' I ask again. 'Sometimes people have to be told things they don't want to hear.'

And then Dr Jago suggests, 'And sometimes people feel better for saying things others do not want to hear.'

'You are a mean pain,' I roar at him. 'How could you say that? I'm telling you, you don't know what the situation was like. You don't know how vulnerable Joel was to these crooks, these shonky shysters with their fraudulent mumbo-jumbo.

'I had to tell him, "It's a cop out, Joel, you're escaping from reality into a world of charlatans, paranormal confidence tricksters parading as superior human beings. They selling illusions, Joel, stop buying their nonsense."

'Joel's expression, I remember, was as cold as a rock face on a winter's day. He showed not a flicker of his soft-hearted personality or his reasoning mind.

' "Flame," he said, "you are trying to put out the light. I can see and believe that there are better planes of living to experience, and you are trying to destroy that hope. I have felt the power of mental energy, of spiritual life that is ours for the asking."

'I tried once more. "Joel," I said, "those crazy people who can apparently curl keys and coil cutlery never allow scientists to thoroughly test their mind power, their effective psychic energy. No, and the reason they don't is that they are greedy frauds making money out of tricks. They are no more than circus magicians.

' "Just imagine," I went on, "if mind-power could really move objects around a room like those floating trumpets, then the world need never have another energy crisis. We could have mentally driven monorails and telepathic Toyotas."

'I thought that was funny, and I started to laugh. But he didn't. He just kept that blank expression, the last expression I ever saw him wear and said, "God knows, and some people have to wait longer than others to find out." '

35

'Not long after this, I met Benji by chance downtown after school,' I tell Dr Jago.

'He asked me, "What can we do to cure Joel for once and for all? His mind seems hooked by that weirdo cult thinking, and it frightens me. He is so ready to believe *anything*."

'I agreed, but I couldn't think of anything. Then I suggested, "Got a few minutes?" He nodded. "Let's ask my friend Lifesaver. He is crazy, but he is clever. I hope he is at home." '

Dr Jago can sense he is in for some important information. He is ready to write notes, dissect my words, my intentions, my mistakes.

I have power over what I tell him, but no power over how he interprets it. Talking is a risky business.

After a long silence, Dr Jago says, 'As you started saying . . .'

'Yes, well,' I continue, 'we located Lifesaver's legs first. They were sticking out from under his ledge, as thin and white as ever.

' "Could be dead," Benji warned, and gave the old boots a kick.

'Lifesaver came out, quite indignant. "Don't kick my good boots. They're marching on to meet up with the diggers that got away." '

'Benji was surprised by the things Lifesaver said, but I wasn't. Benji whispered, "He is crazy, let's get out of here." '

'I ignored Benji and I told Lifesaver about our problem. "We have a friend who believes that there is a better life after death and that there are lots more worlds where intelligences are more developed than ours, and he wants to be part of them." '

' "A far-sighted boy, or a near-sighted boy?" Lifesaver replied.

'I didn't know whether that was a question to be answered or one just to be thought about. You can't always tell with Lifesaver.

'But Benji got straight to the point. "Actually he is blind. We, ah, think it's not healthy for our friend to be so preoccupied, so spaced out with this sort of thinking, and, ah, we were wondering if you could suggest a way to, ah, bring him down to earth." '

' "What does his horoscope tell us?" Lifesaver asked.

' "*Horror*scope!" Benji said, amazed.

' "Nothing to do with horror. No," Lifesaver said, "it is your future as written in the stars. Look into his horoscope and that could put your mind to rest. You will see for yourself cosmic energies affecting his action."

'Lifesaver could not be encouraged to explain any more about this. He went off the air. Benji and I tripped back to that bookshop and found a little booklet titled *Write Your Own Horoscope*. Then we ran back with it to the rock ledge.

'Lifesaver had gone. We crawled under the ledge and read:

Everyone's future is written in the stars. Astrologers can map your life, read your character, know your talents and your future by studying the positions of the stars and planets at the time of your birth.

This map of yourself and your life is called a horoscope. It can be a most revealing document, and a helpful guide when making decisions which affect your future.

All you need to make up your own is found in this booklet.

'Benji and I knew what we had to do. We set about making one up for Joel—one which would make him come to his senses.

'We read on:

A horoscope has three main parts that represent three supposed influences on a person's life. The three parts are: the zodiac (which is a band of stars that circles the earth), the houses, and the planets. Most horoscopes base predictions on the characteristics of the zodiac signs.

'Now, Joel's birthdate is January 22nd. His sign is Aquarius. We looked that up and then added all sorts of silly things which we were sure would open his eyes to the stupidity of it all.'

Dr Jago asks, 'How far did you go with this joke?'

'Joke? Yeah, I suppose we did have a few giggles

about it, especially the plan to get Kate to read it to him, pretending it had been worked out by a professional fortune teller.'

Dr Jago is not impressed. He wouldn't have played a joke, *ever*. I ignore his critical attitude. I continue.

'I took it home and typed it. That took me ages because I can only do it with one finger.

'We gave it to Kate and she said she read it to Joel and he made her read it over and over.

'We watched and waited, hoping he would become more cheerful and positive.'

Dr Jago looks at his watch, intercoms his old bag receptionist and says, 'I'm extending this session with Sally. No interruptions.'

36

Unfortunately, Joel's cat, Lucky, got run over. Everyone felt really sorry for Joel because he seemed to take it so badly. He stayed in his room for days and, I understand, not even Mrs Goldstein could get him to come out.

He did not come with us to the lighthouse the following Sunday arvo. Benji said he tried to persuade him, but Joel said he had things to organise.

Benji felt that he might have upset Joel because he had told him just days before that black cats are super-sensitive since they are living the last of their nine lives. He was joking, trying to cheer him up. Now Lucky was dead, with no chance of another life.

But Joel was not sad for Lucky. He assured Benji that his cat had simply advanced to a higher plane.

'It has now finished with this world—it has been released,' he told Benji.

Just before Benji left for our walk, Joel came out of his room and gave Benji a big parcel.

At first Benji did not know what it was, and he

must have been a bit horrified when Joel said it was Lucky's body. He asked for us to dispose of the package at the exact place where we had tossed the dead bat that windy day.

Joel had wrapped poor Lucky up with so much paper and stuff that she felt as heavy as a dog.

Kate came with us, and, true to her form, she wanted to unwrap the parcel to find out why it was mysteriously weighty. I would not let her.

'Leave the dead alone, Kate,' I told her, 'whatever is in there, Joel wants to put to rest.'

We took it in turns to carry the parcel up the steep track to the lighthouse. Kate complained about the climb, and we told her it would be good for her big behind. She was furious and refused to have anything to do with us when we got to the top.

So we gave her two sandwiches and a soft drink. She sat about fifty metres from us, and stewed.

Benji and I watched her from our favourite hide-out—the cave where we had found the bat. We giggled about the time we invented our blindfold game, and the times we had played it since just as an excuse to touch each other.

We decided not to play it with Kate around because neither of us wanted to feel her big behind!

Then Benji said, 'Remember the first time we played it. Well, Joel told me yesterday that he knew I kissed you. Isn't that amazing?'

Not really, when I think about it. Joel's hearing was so acute that just the little silence when our lips were

161

touching, painted the whole picture for him.

Benji said that our kiss had really hurt Joel and that we shouldn't have done it. He said that he told Joel the kiss was an accident—we just got too close. It could have happened between any two people playing blindfold.

(If that was true, I'm glad we didn't play with Kate. She might have ended up kissing Benji ... by accident?)

Benji then admitted that it was awkward all three of us were such good friends. 'Loving friends' is the way he described us.

'I can't take anything that Joel wants. It wouldn't be right. He started off with so much less. Sometimes I feel guilty. I shouldn't go on dancing if he can only stumble. Flame, you are *my* flame and you are *Joel's* flame. It's hard to be with you, just you and me, together, alone, having fun, when I now know this is what Joel would like.'

For a while, I didn't understand what he was trying to tell me. I hadn't really thought of anything personal between Joel and me, let alone thought out the complications of the different combinations.

Up until this point, it had all been so simple.

But now, yes, I can see that our various relationships, like pieces of a puzzle, made up an impossible picture.

Benji's comments made me realise, or should I say recognise, for the first time that Joel had a crush on me. He had told Benji that loving me was going to prove to be another frustration in his life, that he would

162

never even be able to tell me he loved me, let alone hope that his love would be returned.

And Joel had said that 'obviously I fancied' Benji. How could he get that picture? We never said romantic things. And at a rock concert we went to once, I sat in between them and they both held one of my hands. Truly, we were just kids together, no one left out. Not even Kate.

Benji said it again, 'Flame, you're a blind man's light at the end of his dark tunnel. I must not take that hope, or enjoy your love when it is what my brother wants most.'

I was struck dumb with the magnitude of the problem. I couldn't love Joel in an 'in love' way— he was a 'friend' I loved.

Benji was the one. So many girls would want his kiss, I thought. But, we were still just kids. So silly to be serious. Embarrassing too.

I had to stop that conversation, ignore it, forget it.

'Let's toss Lucky now,' I said, and Kate joined us as we stood at the edge of the cliff near the lighthouse.

We shut our eyes and prayed to God that Lucky, and all the things in the package, be given peace in the everlasting kingdom of Heaven.

37

The person I fear most is Mrs Goldstein, and there she is, waiting outside our house for me to come back from school.

It is months after her first attack on me, but, even now, I just have to close my eyes and I can see her in our kitchen, her flailing arms pounding me like a threshing machine, in the vain hope that grains of truth would fall from my lips.

I should be able to stand up to her now, having been through it all with Dr Jago, but I discover I can't when I turn the corner of our street and see her there, with Mr Goldstein, heading through our front gate, marching towards our front door . . . *again*.

The sight of her sets terror loose inside me. I nip back out of sight before she sees me and scuttle away like a frightened crab in search of a haven of safety.

My mind seemed to be on 'autopilot' as I head towards the beach in desperate need of the comfort and company I am used to finding in that rock shelter.

But Lifesaver is not there. The rock is bare and the seagulls are out fishing.

Back to the main street I go, searching, searching . . . And finally I see him standing in the bus shelter, his head bowed, war medals gleaming on his chest.

'Lifesaver, oh Lifesaver,' I say, 'I need your help. She's waiting for me. She is the mother of . . .'

It is no use, he is not 'at home'. He is deaf to the world around him. He is reciting:

'They shall grow not old, as we that are left grow old,
Age shall not weary them, nor the years condemn,
At the going down of the sun, and in the morning,
We will remember them.'

'Damn you,' I shout at him, but he does not flinch. He is insulated against insult by mental retreat to a peaceful state of mind, where his disturbing memories are obedient to his commands. Like he had explained before, he is in control—he has conquered his nightmares. I have not.

The battle rages within me as I run on, going nowhere in particular, just avoiding the one last ferocious foe I have to face.

My enemy is waiting, patiently, insistently, outside my house in the form of Mrs Goldstein.

I know I must attack her, get it over with, show the world that their deaths were not my fault and must have been *her* fault.

I round the corner of our block, but she is nowhere in sight. I take aim for our front gate. My head feels as if it is wobbling like the knob on the top of a steaming pressure cooker. In that state, human beings can do terrible things. They even kill.

In through the gate, now for the front door. As I open it I hear sobs . . . Tessa's sobs.

I must walk. On. On. There they are together—my mother and their mother, and their father. They stare at me.

Tessa holds out a piece of paper.

'Sally . . . Sally . . . Sally, they found this in Benji's room,' is all Tessa can say.

I take the piece of paper. It is the horoscope Benji and I made up, which I typed out on our rattle-trap machine with the broken keys.

Scrawled across the top from Joel is the message, 'Thanks for this, Benji. I'll be seeing you mate.'

Then there was my handwriting:

> Joel,
> Benji and I got this done for you. Hope you get the hidden meaning.
> love Flame.

Zodiac sign: AQ ARI S

Character: c rio s, odern, o en- inded, o t-going.

And there, in front of my eyes, was all our good advice to Joel: 'You ust take control of yo r life, oel, yo can be reborn. Do not let eo le lead yo astray. Yo are ca able of great self-control. Yo know the right co rse of action, take it.'

Below this, in Kate's handwriting:

166

Missing letters are—P,U,J,M.
And then in Joel's writing:
Code cracked: Message is JUMP.
I think I'm crying out that this is all an accident, 'I meant to fill those letters in by hand. It can't be my fault, it can't be my fault.'

And even louder is Tessa's wailing, 'She didn't mean it, she didn't mean it.'

And high above that, Mrs Goldstein's voice says, 'They jumped on Joel's birthday. Pray he is reborn. Nobody meant their part in it.'

Then we four come together. We hold tight, our pain merges.

We cry together, tears for Benji, tears for Joel, tears for parents, tears for Tessa, and tears for me.

THE END